I0822659

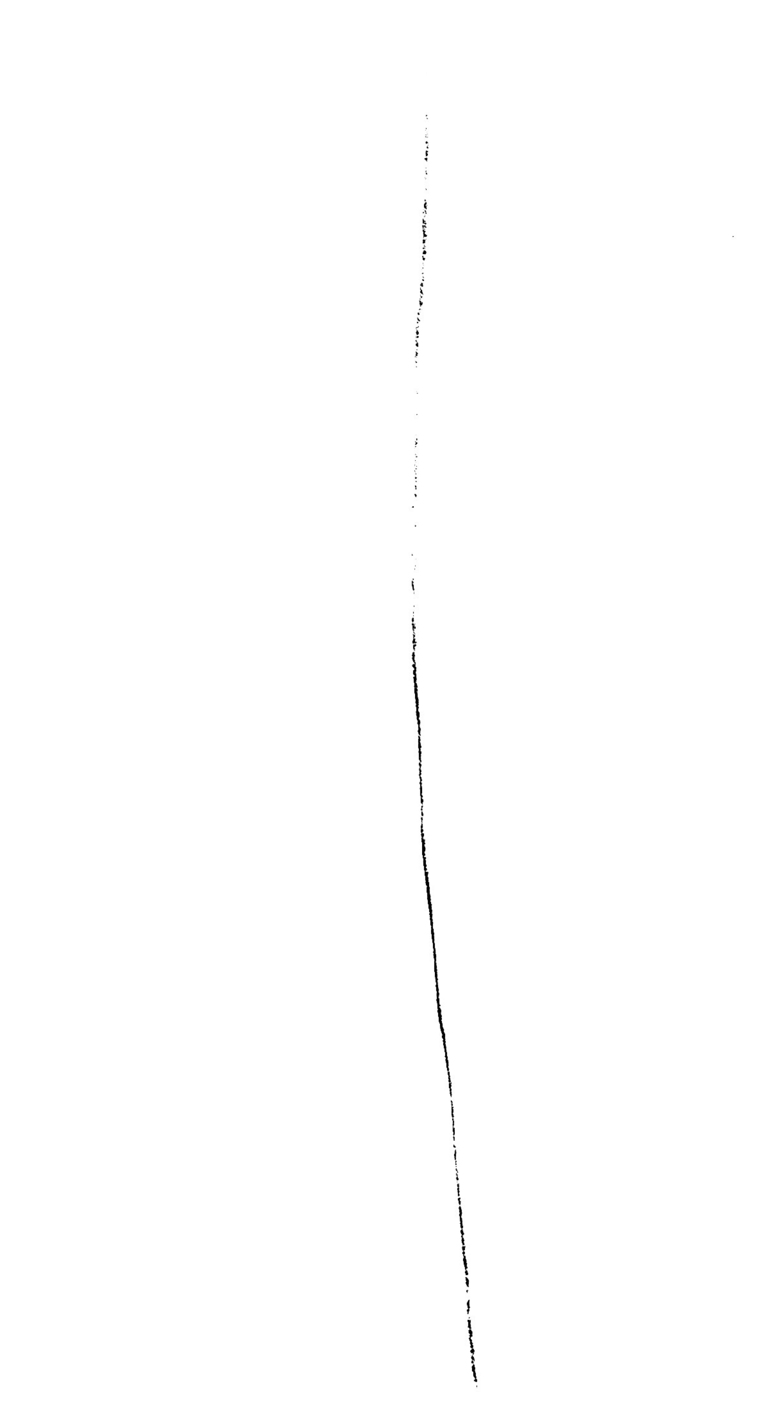

LEIALOHA HUMPHERYS

FALLING FOR THE HUNTSMAN

To Win a Dark Heart

A Villainous Twist on Snow White and Hansel & Gretel

HOKULANI PRESS

This book is a work of fiction. Any references to historical events, real people, or real places are used fictitiously. Other names, characters, places, and events are products of the author's imagination, and any resemblances to actual events or places or persons, living or dead, is entirely coincidental.

First paperback edition April 2026

ISBN (paperback) 978-1-959157-24-3

ISBN (ebook) 978-1-959157-25-0

ISBN (hardcover) 978-1-959157-26-7

Dust Jacket by Leialoha Humpherys

Artwork by EFA Fine Arts

Published by Hokulani Press

Santaquin, Utah

United States of America

www.leialohahumpherys.com

To anyone still making peace with the past.
For the ones learning to let go, forgive, and breathe again.
You deserve to move forward softly, bravely, wholly.
This one is for you.

CHAPTER ONE

ALARIC

They say the sea is cruel, so I learned to be crueler.

The sailor flinched as the hot iron touched his forearm, but I pressed harder. "You steal from my hold, you wear my mark."

He gritted his teeth, and I saw the fury behind his pain.

Good. Let him remember it.

This wasn't punishment. It was justice. A lesson.

Sure, he stole only a little salve for his new, un-trained hands.

But all whalers' hands burned and stained from doing the work we did.

And now, this man would burn for his thievery.

He finally broke, and tears streamed down his face. He had to be about nineteen years of age.

Young, but never too young to avoid accountability.

I threw the brand onto the deck, finding the rest of the whalers still as statues.

They stared wide-eyed.

It'd been a while since I branded a sailor with the "AG" initials of my whaling empire.

"Get back to work," I barked.

No hesitations.

My men flensed the whale, their blades flashing in the moonlight, red and silver. Sharks thrashed near the stern, drawn to the feast. The sea tonight was not blue... but black and crimson with greed.

With five fleets, an empire built on blood and blubber, and enough barrels of whale oil to burn through kingdoms, I had done the unthinkable.

Crowned rulers flinched when they saw my sails on the horizon.

People at every bay and port bowed to my whims.

I had enough gold and treasure to fill all the mansions and palaces in the Tempest Seas.

I should've felt triumphant.

Victorious.

Invincible.

Instead, I stood on the deck and stared into the boiling dark, the scent of burning flesh curling through the salt-drenched air like a ghost.

In the thick of the grime and gore, emptiness.

"That was a fine day," said Destin, my first mate and cousin. He folded his arms, his expression sober. "When they're done, we'll get over three thousand barrels out of all this, Captain."

I nodded, rubbing my jaw.

Three thousand barrels. The yield most men would kill for.

It should've thrilled me.

It didn't.

"Something wrong?" Destin asked.

I glanced at him, the mirror of myself: same dark hair, same sun-worn skin, same calloused hands from a life built on whale blood. We were both twenty-five. Too young to have seen this much death and carnage. Too rich to care.

Still, I'd never tell him.

Or anyone.

"Nothing," I said, turning back to the sea.

"Do you regret not closing the deal with the queen?" Destin asked, prying like a sailor picking apart crab legs for dinner. He knew better than to do this.

I gave him a warning look, enough to put him in place. He took a step back.

"I don't regret anything," I said. Although... my mind wandered to a few days ago, moments before we left the port at Moanalei Kingdom.

The sky hung low, with clouds that foreshadowed a storm.

The port, once so full of life and color, had changed under Sereth's rule.

Guards patrolled the docks, always keeping track of who came and went. They acted like seagulls circling over the sea, looking for something to feed on.

And at that moment, standing at the port not so long ago, the bird's voices wailed across the sky.

Ships groaned against their moorings.

The whole place smelled of rot and grime.

And then there was Sereth, standing beneath a black parasol. Her skin nearly matched the color of her white gloves, her lips the color of blood, and her hair black as ebony. Her cloak billowed in the breeze, dark as a funeral.

But even her beauty could not hide her past.

She had blood on those snow white hands: the blood of her stepmother.

It haunted her eyes. Haunted her kingdom. She couldn't walk anywhere without a guard at her side. Her people feared her. Most had already turned to me for protection, for hope.

But I wasn't a savior. I was a whaler. Not a leader.

Sereth had tried to strike a deal before we set sail: flashing those cold eyes, offering investment in my fleet. She needed my power. My reputation. She wanted to buy back control of her crumbling reign.

No one fooled me.

Everyone was afraid of me, even her. But still... she was fierce. Her armies rivaled the size of my crews. She ruled with an iron hand, a sharp tongue, and the shadow of her own crime behind her.

I could've been that crime.

I'd once sworn to her stepmother that I'd take Sereth to sea, kill her, and toss her overboard.

But I didn't.

And I'd kept one vow ever since: I'd never bow to a crown again. I followed laws, not rulers. I lived on my own terms.

"I don't bow to the queen," I said.

Destin nodded. "I know, Alaric."

"I bow to no one."

"We've spent all our lives hunting though," Destin said and sighed. Was he getting soft? I frowned at him, ready to knock some sense into his skull. He was dreaming again.

It drove me crazy.

"I am a huntsman," I said. "I hunt. And as long as I'm hunting, I am the one in power."

Destin's eyes riveted on the mass below that no longer resembled a humpback, but a carcass with a metallic stench. "No man is too powerful to be hunted, Alaric."

That was enough. I shoved my cousin, and he gasped, but he didn't fight back.

Never did.

He was too loyal.

Instead, he frowned, and before he could speak, I snapped. "*I* am the huntsman, Destin." I slammed my fist on the rail and added, "You are distracted again, cousin. Get that sea witch out of your mind or I will."

Sea witch. Destin fell in love years ago with a mysterious young woman but the witch disappeared.

"At least I have a witch," he muttered.

I cursed and shook my head. I didn't need a witch. I didn't need anyone.

I stormed off.

No man is too powerful to be hunted? Did Destin even realize what I'd built? The power in my hands? I had become so wealthy, so notorious, so large that *nobody* could touch me. Anyone who touched me would be killed.

My men were loyal to me, this business, and this life on the stormy sea.

As I walked onto the helm and took hold of the ship's wheel, I noticed two figures standing to the side. They were tall for teenagers, and very slender. Sereth asked if I might give them safe passage to the kingdom of Corallure, the home of her estranged husband, Elias.

She didn't explain who they were, but paid a handsome sum for their safe delivery. "You must ensure they are promptly taken to the king and queen of Corallure." Sereth had handed me a sealed envelope. "With this," she added. That note was in my quarters now.

Curiosity may have forced anyone else to open it, but I didn't have time or a care for that.

Sereth asked a favor.

She offered good money.

And I said yes.

The teenagers stared at the whale, somber looks in their eyes. The girl then glanced my way, her expression hollow. Her name was Lilo, and, for whatever reason, I felt myself mirrored in her.

A haunted look.

An invisible guard around the soul.

Her twin, Niko, glanced at me too, and it was then I noticed he was holding something. A knife? He fidgeted with it before it disappeared in his fingers. No, his sleeve?

I dismissed it as a hallucination.

Whalers did that a lot, possessed by what we did.

And while we killed, the teens kept to themselves, which I appreciated.

The last thing I needed was to have two troublesome teenagers meddling in my whaling empire.

I frowned, and the twins, who were obviously scared of me like everyone else, quickly redirected their attention to the remnants of the dead whale.

I looked at the sky, finding the stars spread out vast and beautiful. It was peaceful amidst the splashing of the sharks and the cursing and irreverent shanties of my sailors as they flensed the whale.

"Captain!"

I groaned. If there was one more thing we needed to deal with today, someone would get hurt. It was a young sailor, one who had joined our crew recently, if I remembered correctly.

"There's a calf swimming around the ship. It's probably looking for its mother."

The mother...

We killed her.

That was her mass floating in the water as the men finished flensing. If we left the calf alone, it would die a slow, miserable death. Starvation. Slowly nipped to pieces by sharks.

"Kill it," I said.

The boy visibly shrank. I handed him a harpoon. "*You* kill it."

And I followed him.

His fingers shook. He didn't aim properly.

Miss.

The calf swam in circles, dazed and shocked, wailing for its mother.

The boy braced for punishment.

I picked up a bloody harpoon, guiding the boy to finish the job.

"Steady," I said.

I'd done this thousands of times. Trained thousands of men. Killed thousands of whales.

The harpoon let out a soft airy noise as it launched through the air.

The calf struggled.

Then floated.

I turned to the boy. "You miss again, I'll leave you in the water. Understand?"

I didn't even know his name.

He just shuddered. "Aye aye captain."

I returned to the helm and rubbed my temple. The men drew in the dead calf, their harpoons shooting at the sharks before they took all our kill.

The boy looked over the side, his face pale, and he puked.

I closed my eyes, imagining our target destination, Corallure Kingdom. Thinking about the destination always distracted me.

The goal distracted me.

But my thoughts betrayed me.

He's too young for this.

They say the sea is cruel. But cruelty wasn't the hardest part.

It was pretending it never bothered you.

CHAPTER TWO
MALIA

Halekai's farmer's market teemed with locals and visitors alike. Sunshine poured across the terraced town, where handwoven baskets of mangoes, guava, and papaya lined the coastal market like a rainbow.

Thatched umbrellas shaded woven mats and wooden tables stacked with sweet taro buns, glass jars of coconut syrup, and fresh tropical herbs tied with twine.

I moved through the bustle, my boots barely brushing the warm stone as I tried to draw as little attention to myself as possible.

Children darted between vendors, their fingers sticky as they laughed. Aunties called out, selling flower leis and sweet malasadas. Drums and ukuleles echoed from the town square, while the scent of sea and plumerias clung to the breeze.

"Koa bowls!" a man called, and I lowered my head even more, hoping he–with the loud voice–might not notice me. His handmade wooden bowls and other items sat next to a booth with stained glass art. The artists of Corallure were unmatched.

“Get your poke!” said a passing vendor, waving ti leaves to draw people's attention. He pointed them toward his booth and many curious tourists followed him.

I paused, lingering by an old woman’s herb stand. I knew I should keep moving, but it always fascinated me to find other people as interested in herbs and natural remedies as myself.

She had an impressive display of items: sprigs of uhaloa and olena lay bundled beside carved wooden salves. I wished I could get a closer look. My limited eyesight made it impossible to fully examine everything.

Would the old woman perhaps not mind talking to someone like me?

Turning my head, I saw her in my peripheral vision. Engaged with a noblewoman, this old woman seemed well-liked, well-received, and maybe even popular.

She wouldn’t want to be associated with me.

Keep moving, I told myself, and I did.

Everywhere, the market blossomed: bright, warm, familiar. A place I was hoping would feel more like home the longer I lived here.

Except it wasn’t.

I blinked and tried to focus on my steps and avoid bumping into anyone. It was impossible though, with children running around and buyers congregating around certain stands. I kept my head turned to try and capture the images at the edges of my vision, hoping that I could get to my friend before anyone noticed.

Of course that was wishful thinking in such a busy area.

I ran into an older man, who was obviously a whaler based on his cursing. Whaling was illegal in Corallure, but the whaling ships still stopped occasionally for supplies.

He hissed under his breath, “Get out of here, witch!” Fear spread through me like wild mint: quick, invasive, hard to pull out.

I instinctively touched my neck, hoping he didn’t see the burn scars, hoping my hair covered that and my hands.

Hurry, Malia!

I stuck out like a sore thumb with my black dress, and even whalers who weren’t from Corallure could identify me as a witch.

Most of the men wore loose white shirts and vests; most of them whalers, fishermen, and merchants. Their appearance was rough, their skin weathered from the salt and sea, their facial hair and hygiene seemingly unkempt, and their language fouler than the reek of dead fish.

They were a stark difference from the gentlemen-like visitors who came from Moanalei or other parts of Corallure Kingdom. The gentlemen wore suits and crisp white shirts under them. They would dab sweat on their foreheads with their handkerchiefs.

And beside the gentlemen were gentlewomen, parasols in hand. In the heat of the day, they wore long-sleeved blouses and wide-brimmed hats, their skirts covering their well-laced boots. Some wore elegant corsets and vibrant-colored skirts, matching the tropical world around us.

Many of them wore their hair in elegant updos and spiraled curls, while my hair hung long and straight down my back. I moved cautiously, keeping in the shadows of the covered booths, then standing behind people or the twisted branches of banyan trees to check my surroundings before going into any open areas.

A child ran straight into my legs, and I almost dropped

my basket of goods. When I looked down, I could not see the child's face. As had been my vision since a young age, there seemed to be a dark, blurry mass in the center of my focus. I had to turn my head, looking out of the corners of my eyes in order to see him.

And even at that, it'd take me a moment to really look before getting the details of his face: the color of his eyes, the shape of his nose...

Faces and expressions were difficult to make out, but I heard him before I could read his face.

He screamed. "It's the witch!"

Heart racing, sweat sticking in the palms of my hand, I hurried past the child and the crowd, hoping I would find Noni soon. This was my first time doing this.

And maybe my last. Perhaps this was a bad idea...

I hated that my eyes *looked* normal. Maybe it would be better if they had a grayish film or something that could help people see I had an eyesight disability.

But no. That I had normal-looking eyes only stoked the rumor about being a witch. "She looks fine," people would say, "So she must be hiding something."

I passed a stand with women who looked more like myself.

I must be getting closer to Noni. She usually hung out with the locals.

The native women of the island–with dark hair and light brown skin like myself–wore plain dresses, but not black. They grew quiet as I passed.

I pretended it didn't bother me.

People here didn't trust me, as if I were a toxic side effect of a potion. They didn't like that I was different, and most days I wished I could hide away forever.

But perhaps there was something deep inside of me

that hoped maybe... just *maybe*... I could drop off some goods at the farmer's market and the people who bought them might start welcoming me as their own...

Perhaps it's just wishful thinking, I told myself. *I'm a witch.*

I was the witch with long hair and black dresses, who lived in a black cottage in the woods a safe distance from the quaint town of Halekai. What other colors was I expected to wear and use? Besides, when I *had* gone to a seamstress a few months ago, having saved up enough money for a new dress, she told me the only thing I'd be able to get from her was a black dress.

"Suits a witch like you," she said. Out of spite, I took her up on the offer.

Out of spite... I rolled my eyes as I pushed on through the busy market. *More like I had no other choice.* She was the best–priced seamstress in town and the only one who would do business with me. It was ridiculous that I'd come from a life of wealth and luxury to this life of poverty and ostracization.

"Watch where you're going," a well-dressed woman snapped at me as I accidentally brushed her shoulder.

It was late afternoon, and already some vendors were closing up for the day. I worried I had arrived too late, but the area was so packed, I told myself I still might sell the baked goods I'd brought.

I caught sight of Noni, a friend who offered to sell my goods at her booth. She was a kind woman, and someone I'd met when, in desperation, her husband came to me asking for help. Noni had just given birth and had a raging fever. Her husband went to every doctor and medicine man in town, but each told him Noni wouldn't make it.

With my knowledge of herbs and medicines, I could help her.

We'd been friends ever since.

"Aloha, Aunty Malia!" One girl ran up to me, clutching my dress and jumping up and down. I crouched to hug her, warmth filling my empty soul. It was warmer than any cup of herbal tea. What a joy to be called an aunty!

And as the little girl hugged me, a bittersweetness came over me of the fact I'd never have children of my own. I'd never have a family of my own. Because nobody would ever see past the monster I was...

I was like a weed in a garden of beautiful flowers: *very* unwanted.

Malia... I warned myself, not wanting to drown in those thoughts.

Not now.

"There you are! I was worried you weren't coming," said Noni, and we kissed one another's cheeks. She looked me up and down, and I saw the silent skepticism in her eyes. Though we were friends and quite amiable with one another, we were not close.

She still had her questions and doubts about me, especially my being a witch. Noni had been bold enough to ask me questions about my past–something nobody else had ever done–but I was too afraid to tell her.

I skimmed over the truth and then gave up. "It's better that you don't know," I said.

"But people can find out that you're not a wicked witch!" Noni had fought back. "You're just good with herbs–"

"I *am* a herb witch," I had corrected her, and that was the end of that conversation.

Like the other women, Noni wore a long-sleeved white blouse tucked into a dark brown skirt, and her koa colored hair was down today, like mine. On her table sat jars of fresh honey. She and her family ran a beekeeping business, and locals and visitors alike would buy her goods like the swarming bees Noni cared for. I always had to ask her to save a jar for me because she ran out so quickly.

The addition of my banana bread and ginger snaps was a great idea, and I finally caved, hoping that selling my goods might make me a few extra coins, something I could always use. I did odd jobs here and there, making medicine for people, but I hoped to one day have a more sustainable job... if only my reputation as a witch didn't precede me...

"Aue, don't grab your sister's hair!" Noni snapped at one of her children then let out a breath before returning her attention to me. "Did you bring the goods?"

"Yes." I barely opened my basket, the aroma of banana bread and gingersnap cookies filling the air, when someone spoke from behind.

"That smells incredible. What is that?"

Noni and I turned to see a young man. Noni curtsied, and it took me a second longer to make out his features. His regal attire and the crown on his head signified that he was the prince of Corallure Kingdom, Elias. He was handsome, with light chestnut brown hair, blue eyes, and tanned skin. He had always been very kind when I'd met him several times. But he'd been especially kind when I first sought refuge here. Despite his compassion, there was also a distance in his emotions.

Even now, he tipped his head to us and smiled, but the smile never reached his eyes. Something haunted him...

Her.

He motioned to my basket. "May I see?"

"Of course." I pushed it towards him, watching as he examined the contents. "You're welcome to try," I added, and when he took a bite, he seemed to melt just a little.

"Wow Miss Malia, those are so good."

Miss Malia. Noni gave me a suspicious look. How did the prince know my name? I swallowed hard, hoping she would not ask.

Prince Elias nodded. "I'm sure my father and Damien would love to try some of this too. They don't get out much." Damien was the Crown Prince, Elias's older brother. And Elias's father, King Halstead, was a good and benevolent king. If every kingdom had a ruler like him, the world would be a much better and kinder place. Corallure had its faults, like the lack of border control, the overbearing tourism industry, and the rigid class system, but it was much better than Moanalei...

For me at least.

If only I could live in a wooden cottage here in town, surrounded by the colorful roofs, cozy homes, and view of the cream-colored palace in the distance.

But for now–and maybe the rest of my life–I had to be content hiding.

Perhaps in time people would accept me.

King Halstead set the tone for his kingdom, and while people still didn't trust me and a nasty rumor got around that I was a witch who "ate children," I would still rather live here than back at Moanalei, my homeland.

Prince Elias was the only person here who did not look at me like a witch and who did not hesitate before trying something to see if it was poisoned, cursed, or spelled... I felt grateful for that. I wouldn't say we were close or anything, but there was an unspoken understanding between us.

We had both dealt with *her*, and the hurt from her actions was something we shared, a poison that ran through the veins of our past. Though, I was sure his heartache must run deeper than mine.

He'd been married to Sereth, the queen some people called Snow White.

A clinking noise distracted me from my thoughts as the prince handed me a little bag of coins.

"Oh, that's too much–" I began to say, but he ignored me.

"How often do you bring these baked goods to the market?" he asked.

"Today is my first time trying." I smiled nervously, trying to make sure my face was in his direction, but hating that I couldn't see his face when I looked directly at him. "And you're my first customer."

Elias laughed, but it sounded hollow. Everything about him felt like the ghost of someone who once was, and my heart hurt for him. "Well what a treat–literally."

Noni laughed at his joke, and while there was a lightness in the conversation, there was a secret heaviness, a burden that he and I shared, and one that felt like a festering wound that would never heal.

The prince bought a jar of honey from Noni, then went on his way.

"How did he know you?" Noni folded her arms. "You never told me you knew the prince personally–"

"Oh there's nothing personal," I quickly said, but my voice cracked as I rushed to place the rest of my baked goods on her table.

"If he weren't still married to that Moanalei queen, I'd say you two should court," Noni said, and I gave her a look.

"No, no, no. I'm *not* looking for any kind of relationship."

I didn't want to say, "He's royalty, and I'm a commoner..." because then I'd be lying. Sure, I hid a lot about my past, but I certainly was not a liar.

"Why not? You match! I won't pretend I haven't noticed your strange ways, Malia. But not in a witchy way. You walk and act like a princess." She laughed, then added, "You speak as refined as a princess!"

I paled. Had she figured it out?

But Noni was too busy talking. "And besides your unusually refined way of speaking for an *herb witch*, you're... how old now? Twenty two? Time to find a man and settle down. Besides, you made him laugh! I don't think I've seen the prince laugh or smile since he came back." Noni placed her hands on her hips and raised an eyebrow. I blushed.

"It's truly nothing like that, Noni. He and I... we just..." I let out a breath, unable to explain myself.

Noni then motioned around us. "Fine, but there are whalers all around here–handsome ones! Why don't you find yourself a catch?" She winked.

"Noni." I rolled my eyes, and she laughed. But her words about the prince made my heart ache even more for him. If only people understood what he'd gone through–what I'd gone through.

"Whalers are *not* for me." I shook my head. "I would never fall for a whaler. Besides, I'm perfectly fine hiding out at my cottage." I quickly added, "Alone."

Noni studied me. Her expression softened. "You can't hide forever, Malia."

A lump formed in my throat. What did Noni know about hiding? Her life had never been at risk, and she hadn't made the awful mistakes that I'd made...

When I didn't reply, Noni took a small breath then arranged the banana loaves and ginger snaps on her table. After a moment, she gazed at me, a softer look spreading on her face. “You should bake more goods for the farmer’s market tomorrow, and if it continues to go well, we should keep doing this at every market.”

Warmth filled me, something I hadn’t felt in a while. “Alright, that’s a great idea.” I loved baking. The prince had bought my goods. Noni was sure they would continue to sell. Their confidence in me filled me with a sense of purpose.

“I’ll bake tonight and bring more in the morning,” I said, and Noni nodded.

“Sounds great. You'd better hurry home though. Storm is rolling in.”

I looked at the skies and, indeed, a storm seemed to approach, the clouds gray and heavy. Hopefully, there were no ships out in that weather.

I thanked Noni for selling my baked goods, kissed her cheek goodbye, then made my way out of the busy Halekai port town. I veered off the path and traversed deep into the woods, glad for the sunlight so I could find my way. The sound of people chattering and the hustle of the town disappeared, replaced by the hum of the waves on the shore, and the rustling of the leaves in the coconut fronds above.

A cool breeze blew through the woods. Corallure was a tropical island, yes, but it was quite cool and rainy most of the year. It was cool enough that on some nights, one could see their breath in the air. I loved it, but secretly missed the warmth of Moanalei.

When I reached my cottage, I let out a breath of relief. The sun set on the ocean horizon, and a smile crossed my face. A whale breached in the distance, a reminder of hope.

A promise.

But a rumbling of thunder filled the sky and squashed

that hope. I pulled out my ingredients for a late night baking session, knowing that the smell would probably fill the air.

But it's alright, I told myself, always cautious of not drawing attention to myself. *Nobody is out at this hour.* It was just me. All alone. Hiding.

Because, unlike Noni suggested earlier, I was sure I *could* hide forever.

CHAPTER THREE
ALARIC

"All hands on deck!" Destin bellowed over the rumble of thunder.

I stood at the helm, one hand on the wheel, eyes locked on the storm swelling ahead. It didn't look terrible... yet. But I'd weathered too many tempests to trust a quiet sky or calm waters.

The sea turned without warning. And when she turned, she didn't care who crossed her path.

As the men scrambled to their positions, I caught sight of the twins, pale and white-knuckled, peering over the edge of the deck.

"Below deck," I said flatly.

They turned, startled, those hollowed eyes filled with terror.

"Stay down. Don't come back up unless I say."

They didn't argue. Just nodded and vanished, boots pounding toward the hatch.

"Captain," Thatcher called, climbing the steps toward me, soaked to the bone but steady as ever. "Corallure's not far. If we cut southwest and hold course, we'll beat the worst of it to port."

He was only the same age as me. Young, but he never guessed. Thatcher did math like he was born for it. If he said we had it in us to get through it, we probably could.

"Good," I said, eyes still on the sky. "Hold to it."

Lightning split the clouds overhead. In the electric lighting, I thought I saw the shape of a whale tail in the distance, sinking slowly beneath the sea. It looked strangely more white than other whale tails I'd ever seen in my life. I rubbed my eyes. Was I imagining things?

Focus, Alaric.

Rain sheeted across the deck, and the panic among the men moved like a wave.

Not shouting. Not chaos. Just that sharp, quiet tension when every sailor knew the sea was about to test them.

"Steady, boys," I said, not even a shred of fear in my heart. "We're close."

And just like that... we moved on.

THE SILENCE WAS SO LOUD, my heart beat in my ears like cannons and gunpowder. It was a sensation I wasn't used to, and one I did not welcome. The sails of my beloved ship, the Crimson Wake, hung in shreds. Every part of the ship ached and groaned, beaten and defeated from the storm.

It would take at least a week in Corallure to get her back into top shape.

All of the men moved like walking corpses, having done everything to fight the storm and keep the ship from turning over or getting caught off course.

The rain and the waves ripped through every seam, and every heart.

Lilo and Niko had since returned to the deck, their movements restless.

It was nearing midnight, and since passing the storm, it was eerily quiet, as if the waves were too tired to make noise.

I looked overboard to find the full moon reflected.

"Thatcher!" I called, and the bright blonde came running.

"Yes sir?"

"How close are we?"

"Not too far. We should see the lighthouse any minute now, Captain."

I squinted ahead of us, knowing that somewhere... in that midst of darkness, there was an island, home to King Halstead and Queen Charlotte and their two sons, Crown Prince Damien and Prince Elias... the same prince that was married to Sereth but walked away from her years ago.

"Alaric!"

I frowned and turned to Destin. He only used my first name, as opposed to "Captain" or "Sir," when he was really worried about something. The storm was over. What could he possibly be worried about now? A hole in the brig? Did we lose someone overboard? Everyone had been accounted for...

"What now?"

"Alaric, someone's following us."

I frowned and looked behind the ship.

Pitch blackness. "How can you tell?"

"They've snuffed their lights but I caught sight of them just a few minutes ago."

"Merchants?" I asked.

"It's too dark to see any coat of arms... or anything, really," Destin said. "But I have a bad feeling about it."

I stared into the darkness, rubbed my chin, and nodded. "Me too."

I heard of Corallure ships patrolling their seas like hungry vultures. Whaling was illegal for miles off their shores.

Their whale supply was incredible. If we could hunt here, we'd never have to go to far off remote seas.

The Corallure King paid handsome sums to anyone who caught illegal whalers and brought them to him. So merchants would often patrol the shores, hoping to catch illegal hunters.

But we're not whaling. Furthermore, it was the dead of night...

I suddenly turned to Destin. "Do you hear that?"

"What?" He listened.

Water lapped onto the sides of another ship, brushing its wooden planks, teasing us like a shark circling its prey.

"Look." I frowned as a dark silhouette emerged from the starboard stern. It was sleek, lean, and closing fast. "That's no pirate nor merchant," I said.

It was too well-kept.

The boards were stained to perfection.

The bow had a well-carved mermaid, unmarred by time at sea.

Every inch of the ship was decorated with filigree and gold foil.

This ship belonged to royalty.

And then I saw it: the orange sun flag of Corallure Kingdom. What were they doing out here at this hour? And with no lights?

Before I could shout orders, the ship turned broadside.

"Brace for impact!" The firing of cannons drowned my words.

Boom! Boom! Boom!

There was no time to react.

Wood splintered the air.

Fire erupted.

Oil spilled from barrels left on the deck.

The Crimson Wake lurched and shuddered under the impact. Several of my men were sprawled out, injured from the first cannons. Blood hit the deck before wood or oil.

My ears rang from the noise, but I was already moving and shouting orders. Grappling hooks clanged against the gunwale, and ropes flew.

My insides tightened.

They're coming for us.

Figures in dark coats swung across the ravine, their boots landing on the deck with hard thuds. And that's when I knew: these truly were not merchants *or* pirates.

They were assassins. The men with dark coats wore bandannas over their noses and mouths to mask their identities, and they carried swords, immediately inflicting death to any in their path. I did a quick glance around to find the twins.

Nowhere in sight. Hopefully they stayed below deck.

"Boarders!" I exclaimed. "To arms! Repel them!"

Chaos ensued. Steel clashed against steel. Men screamed.

Fighting.

Cannons exploding.

A *whoosh* sounded in the air and suddenly, a lick of flames consumed the whale oil that spilled on the deck. And despite all the commotion, one assassin fixed his attention on me.

He was the tallest and leanest of the bunch, with a harpoon strapped to his back.

My expression hardened. *We've met before.*

And then I was running towards him, sword drawn. It was almost as if time reversed and an event from a few years ago resurfaced. I had been young, but my future was promising. I was quickly growing in esteem, power, and wealth, and I had just sealed a deal to own a fleet of old ships being sold by a retiring whaler.

It was then that this same assassin had tried to knife me while I walked alone at the port.

He would've succeeded had Destin and Thatcher not come to my aid.

I'd never learned the man's name, nor his motives. But I did learn one thing: I had enemies, people who wanted me dead.

It didn't matter to me who it was.

I had made many enemies on my path to owning this empire. People coveted my wealth, my power. I'd been cruel to many men, and many men walked away in bitterness and anger.

But this assassin... there was something about him that felt off.

Desperation.

Desperation clung to him like salt after a long voyage. Couldn't explain it, but he moved like a man possessed by something.

Another cannon exploded, and the ship made a cracking sound while tipping dangerously starboard. It was the sound and movement that meant only one thing: the ship was sinking.

We can still salvage it, I thought. If Corallure was close enough, the men could board the damage. We could drag her to port and get the repairs it needed...

The assassin started towards me, but then something caught his attention.

He froze.

It was then I noticed the twins standing by the hatch that led below deck, their faces white with fear. The ship lurched to the side again, and I grasped the railing, not giving it a second thought.

I made a promise to deliver them safely to Corallure.

The man had already started making his way towards them. Why? I leaped off the helm and blocked him, our swords clashing.

More cannons fired. The stench of burning whale oil filled the air, and it finally lit.

"Get out of here!" I yelled at the kids.

Now that I was on deck, it was like being enveloped in a battlefield.

Wounded and dead sailors were strewn across the deck. My heart fell. How many men had died tonight? They'd weathered the storm, but not this... this was cold-blooded murder....

An aching sense of dread tugged at me, reminding me I was responsible for their deaths. This was my crew. These were my men.

"Thatcher!" I yelled as I fought off the assassin. "Get us on course!"

And my navigator ran to the helm.

"Get the captain!" said another assassin.

The first blade came for my throat.

I ducked, twisted, and drove my shoulder into the attacker's gut, hearing the grunt of surprise as he staggered back. Two more closed in fast.

Black-clad, faces masked, eyes like glass. Assassins. Five of them.

My sword was already in hand. I slashed one across the thigh and elbowed another in the jaw hard enough to hear the crack. The fight turned savage, fast. One moved like a shadow behind me.

I pivoted just in time, parrying his curved blade with a clang that rattled my bones.

Too slow.

Pain flared white-hot at my side. The leader had slipped past my defenses and slashed me deep. The sting was ice and fire all at once, my ribs screaming with it.

I staggered but didn't fall.

Blood soaked my shirt, warm and steady. I roared, lashed out, and knocked him back with the hilt of my blade.

Another lunged.

I spun, kicked him in the chest, and sent him sprawling. My vision blurred, but I kept fighting. I couldn't stop. I wouldn't stop.

Another attacker, down.

Another, gone.

Only one remained, the tall desperate leader, circling like a wolf.

But I bled too fast. My breath came out ragged, my strength slipping like water through cracked fingers. I raised my blade one last time.

He didn't strike again. He looked at me, nodded once like I'd earned it, then vanished into the night.

I fell to one knee, clutching my side. The scent of iron filled my lungs.

I'd been stabbed before. Cut. Beaten.

But this... this felt final.

A bell rang in the distance. Lights shone on the water.

And then Thatcher rang our bell.

A distress call.

I glanced at the lights. Corallure Kingdom. They rang out their bell, calling to us.

We were close. So, *so* close.

Is it safe to port there though? If they were trying to attack us, then why were they offering help?

And why were these Corallure assassins fleeing when they were so close to the port?

I looked around at my ship. My heart sank, my breaths shallow, as I saw the unmoving bodies around me. Why did the Corallure ship attack without confronting us first?

Things didn't add up.

Except one: *They sent someone to kill me.*

I took off my hat, tipped my chin to the fallen, and then slowly, achingly made my way to the helm.

My men needed order. Leadership.

Every part of my body protested, but I had to move.

"Captain!" Destin yelled.

His voice was frantic, but I didn't react quickly enough.

And that was when it happened... there was another round of cannons fired.

The last round.

Aimed right at me.

The ground exploded beneath my feet and I flew into the air.

As fire, wood, debris, smoke, and oil consumed me, I knew I'd be going to the locker this time.

My body hit the waves, my consciousness failing me.

Water filled my lungs.

I knew I needed to swim, but my body protested. It seemed I was in my body, but I could not tell it what to do.

Shock... I was in shock. Several more booming noises sounded above the surface, and planks of wood, barrels, and metal fell into the water.

The pieces brushed past me.

I had never really imagined dying, perhaps because I'd always been so invincible, so untouchable. It would take a miracle to survive this.

And now that death had come, the strangest feeling ripped out my heart: Regret.

Regret at having lived the life I dreamed of yet not enjoying it.

Regret at all the darkness in my past: teaming up with a wicked queen to kill her daughter, pretending like it didn't bother me, pretending that my whaling empire could make up for such an almost-heinous deed...

And so much more.

I was too delirious to picture all the regret, but it was all there, piercing me like a harpoon striking a whale.

I'm gone, I thought, sinking.

Drowning.

This was the end of Alaric Galeborne, the wealthiest, most powerful whaler in all the seas. He died just like any other whaler, returning to the sea he thought he conquered.

And then something happened... something *moved.* It rose beneath me. Not wood. Not man.

Flesh.

Huge.

Living.

My fingers found something solid. It was skin slick with seawater, something that wasn't slimy but warm with life. I clung to the fin, my nails scraping across barnacle-crusted bumps, and felt the powerful muscle shift beneath me as the whale moved.

I was delirious. Dying. This couldn't be real.

Yet, it lifted me toward light, where I coughed salt and

blood. The world bobbed around me and a blowhole exhaled, misting the air. More cannons sounded somewhere, but my ears were ringing, and I could barely make out my ship, the Crimson Wake, lighting the night sky in the distance. My final thought was in concern for my men. Were they alright? I hoped that they and the Crimson Wake would make it to the port before sinking.

The whale swam, and, I, half-dead, floated above the deep in the arms of a beast my harpoon had hungered for.

I was saved by the very creature I killed.

SAND.

I clutched it, dragging myself onto shore. Waves broke around me, and a light rain fell. The world was pitch black.

I gasped for air, trying to get my bearings.

Every inch of my body protested against movement, but I was alive.

Alive.

The sound of the blowhole filled the air behind me.

I looked, though knives pierced my side, at the last sight of the whale. All I saw was its tail, disappearing below the surface. It had an unusually white tail for a humpback whale, but I was hallucinating. Or was I?

I scanned the area, knowing that if I didn't get help now, I would die here.

My blood curled in rage against the Kingdom of Corallure, no doubt whose island I was on at this very moment. And that anger fueled me to move.

I had to get help.

Had to get back to my crew.

I rose to my feet, clutching my side, each breath labored as I hobbled across the sand and into the forest.

It was then I smelled something.

Warmth. Sweetness. Coziness.

Nostalgia filled me with memories of sitting in my mother's kitchen as a little boy.

It smelled like bananas and ginger and everything good in this world.

And that was when I saw the light. It flickered in the woods, like a lighthouse beckoning to me. It felt dreamlike. Had I died and now found myself approaching my mother?

I dragged myself to the cottage. Pounded on the door.

The feel of the hardwood against my knuckles told me this was real, not a dream.

Even despite my consciousness fleeing in and out like the tide.

"Help!" I exclaimed, knocking again, my knees giving out. I fell to the ground, still clutching my side. Blood soaked my shirt like stain clinging to wood in the sun.

Someone *had* to be here. The smell of baking gave it away.

Then the door opened. It was just a crack, but the sweet, comforting aroma filled the air. It was so refreshing and wonderful, it caused a stir of hope inside of me. If this were the last thing I experienced before dying, that wouldn't be such a bad way to go out.

A chain sounded, and the door opened fully. A young woman stood there, curtains of black hair falling down either side of her face. She knelt down, her eyes wide, but her head was turned, as if she was looking away.

"You're a whaler, aren't you?" she asked.

I nodded, and her expression hardened. Thunder rolled above.

I tried to get up, but the wound at my side caused a ripping sensation through my body.

The world around me turned black.

I'm going to die, I thought, staring at the face of the young woman.

She's very beautiful, came the next thought. She looked like an angel... an angel who seemed to look past me. But, honestly, if she was the last person I saw before dying, that wasn't such a bad way to go out either.

CHAPTER FOUR
MALIA

A *whaler.*

A good-for-nothing whaler.

Here was a man with the blood of innocent creatures on his hands.

I rubbed my eyes as I paused next to the settee and studied the man's face, my own face turned to get the best possible look at him. He was quite handsome, a fact that annoyed me more than I thought it would.

When he knocked earlier, my heart pounded, like it was being smothered in a mortar and pestle. Who would beg for entrance at a midnight hour?

Is it her? That was all I could ask myself.

For a moment, I was sure I'd been found. Panic washed over me, stinging like alcohol on a wound.

She found me...

I paced back and forth a few times, but nobody knocked again. So I opened the door and peeked out. The aroma of banana bread and gingersnaps mixed with the welcome smell of rain.

Instead of standing face to face with someone, I looked down to find a man there, half dead.

Who is he? I asked as I checked his body. *What happened to him?* The gouge on his side bled profusely, and debris coated his skin.

And underneath it all, he was clearly a man of the sea. Big. Brawny. Skin stretched from the sun like leather.

Which meant one thing: He was actively involved. He had probably killed many, *many* whales.

If I save him, I thought, *He'll just kill more whales.* But I was not about to let a human die, because I thought the life of an animal was more important...

Besides, I have to save him, I told myself. *Or everyone will think I'm the monster I am...*

So I dragged him in, cleaned and sewed up his wound. The stitches weren't perfect, but they were impressive for my limited eyesight. I washed his body as best I could and got him comfortable on the settee. I would have to apologize later, because I had to remove his soiled, bloody clothing, but I tried to keep him modest and dignified.

The fireplace roared while the storm rattled off outside, and I scrubbed any blood and debris that had accumulated on the floor. As I got closer to the settee and to the stranger on it, I took a shaky breath.

What if he's sent by her? Was I housing a man who would kill me once he recovered?

I slipped a piece of his dark hair from his forehead. And though a little pale from the loss of blood, he already looked much better, his breathing steady and his expression peaceful.

Don't be silly, Malia. He was wounded. Something had happened, and he washed up on the shores here. I'd even heard the bells of a ship in the distance.

Perhaps this man was a lone survivor of the storm that had just passed. Or perhaps there was something darker at work.

Only time will tell.

HE DIDN'T WAKE up fully for a few days. Each time he did, though, I'd try to feed him and tend to him. I helped him to the washroom where he could relieve himself. I'd wait for him, but he was so weak from the short walk, he'd collapse on the settee afterward and sleep for hours on end. He was terribly dirty and needed a proper bath, but we'd have to figure that out later.

The main thing was that the biggest wound on his side was clean, neatly stitched up, and healing.

One night, as I knelt by him, trying to clean the wounds on his face, he woke. Fully woke. I gasped, reeling back as our eyes locked, as far as I could tell. He tried to sit up, causing me to push him back down. "Don't move–" I said, but he grit his teeth in pain, even flinching at my touch.

Like a true whaler, the first thing he did was curse. I bit back a harsh word about *not* using profanity in my home and, instead, focused on helping him relax.

"You're alright, but you need to rest," I said.

"Where am I?" he asked, delirious. His voice was smoky and low, and his dark brown eyes studied me. His eyes settled on the burn marks covering my neck and hands. Then they returned to my face. "Are you the angel who saved me?"

I blushed. "No. I'm not an angel, but I will help you get better."

"With a face like that, you're too pretty to be from down here."

I frowned. If he were thinking clearly, he'd notice my black dress and that I most certainly didn't look like an angel. The burn marks should've raised some concern for him too.

He's delirious. And he needed rest.

The whaler started to move again when I gently pushed him.

"Please..."

His skin was warm to the touch, and it was quite awkward that he wasn't wearing a shirt... or anything for that matter. A large blanket covered him, but still.

"Listen," I said. "You need to rest, and when you're feeling better, we'll figure everything out."

"What's your name?" he asked, though he already began to fall asleep again. His temperature was too high. He needed rest.

"I don't normally share my name with strangers," I said softly.

He raised an eyebrow as if he found that amusing. "My name's Alaric. Alaric Galebourne. Now that you know who I am, I would say we aren't strangers anymore. Would you?"

I gaped.

Alaric Galebourne, the wealthiest, most reputable whaler in all the Tempest Seas? What was *he* doing *here*, washed up like driftwood?

His steady breaths meant he'd fallen asleep again. My stomach tightened as I continued gently cleaning his wounds.

He killed so many whales. Commanded fleets. Supplied whale oil to every kingdom, island, and province.

And here he was.

I loved whales, and it hurt that they were being

destroyed at such a rapid rate. And the man in charge of their murders was here. On my settee.

My mind raced. He had to go as soon as possible.

I WENT off to the farmer's market the next morning, wondering if I'd hear any gossip about Alaric Galebourne or his ship. Not surprisingly, I found a new crew of whalers. They looked rough, just as Alaric had.

Like they'd seen battle.

Battle... Yes. That would explain all the debris on Alaric's skin and his gaping wound.

I thought of going up to them but lingered in the shadows of the banyan trees, changing my mind. With big, brawny bodies and rough, hardened expressions, they were the face of intimidation. I shrank and went around them to find Noni.

"Did you notice those whalers?" I asked as I placed my baked goods on her table. She nodded and leaned in.

"Heard their ship came to port badly beaten. It's one of Galeborne's crews."

Not just *one* of his crews. It was *his* crew.

And what if they mutinied against him? If I told them where he was, would they come to my cottage to finish the job?

I had no answers until Alaric fully woke.

What was I to do until then? Well...

I reviewed everything I knew or heard about Alaric Galeborne: He was from Moanalei Kingdom. He was the famous huntsman who saved Sereth's life from her "wicked" stepmother. And since that day, his fame only grew until he became the most feared and powerful whaler in all of Tempest Seas.

I thought about telling Noni, but decided that the less she and others knew about me, the better. What if they knew my connection to Sereth and Moanalei Kingdom by realizing my fears about Alaric and his ties to her? Then my hiding place would be revealed, and Sereth might come after me.

I can't risk it.

So I stumbled back to my cottage, basket full of food and clothes for Alaric. With the whaler's condition, he might be here *very* long, a thought that filled me with dread.

When I opened the door, Alaric tried to sit up, his eyes on me. But he grimaced in pain and grabbed his side. Another line of curses fell from his lips and, this time, I gave him a look.

"You're in my home now, and in my home, you will not use filthy whaler's profanity."

His hardened expression softened, but only for a moment, where he winced and looked down, an expression of disgust on his face. He was obviously not used to being told what to do. He submitted anyway. He had no choice but to. "Very well, Ginger."

"Ginger?"

"It's what I'm calling you since you won't tell me your name."

I placed my basket on the counter. My cottage was small, with a kitchen on one side and a small living space on the other. A door led from the living space to my bedroom and washroom. "Why Ginger?"

"Because your house smells like gingerbread." He took a shaky breath, and almost immediately, I knew he was hungry. He wouldn't say it–after all, this wasn't his home, and he depended completely on me. Alaric tried to sit up again, but let out a desperate breath and lied back down.

"It was deep," I said, handing him some clothes. "You should rest as much as you can for the first few days." He took the clothes, but he didn't look embarrassed. If anything, he seemed annoyed that he was so vulnerable. "I'm not sure if they'll fit," I said, "but I gave it my best guess." At that, I entered my kitchen and began preparing a stew. The huntsman, no doubt, had to be starving, and the sooner I got him fed, healed, and out of here, the less he would know about me.

He groaned quietly as he changed, but I gave him his space and wouldn't look. After a moment of silence, I dared glance into the living room. He sat up, his face pale from the effort, and his fingers clutching the edge of the settee. His shirt was off, a smart move on his part. If he put it on, I'd only have him take it off again to tend the wound.

But, for whatever reason, my stomach tightened at the sight of him. I'd seen men without their shirts before but my... he was quite muscular. He'd been lying down most of the time with a blanket on him, and, when I helped him to the washroom to relieve himself, he wore the blanket around his body. But now, seeing him sit up, and very much alive...

It was slightly terrifying and intriguing at the same time.

Malia! I returned my attention to the batch of fresh baked rolls I'd whipped. An island breeze wafted through the cottage and a light rain pattered again outside. The noise was soothing, and I tried to focus on that feeling rather than the anxiety knotting in my stomach about Alaric's presence.

"Here, eat." I handed the whaler his bowl, then sat on

the rocking chair. He watched me for a moment, and when I took a bite, he took his. It was quite... sweet of him to wait for me to eat first.

Very gentlemanlike, I thought, but shoved it away. Whalers were *not* gentlemen.

Alaric ate slowly, his breaths shaky. No doubt any movement in his upper body affected the wound.

"What happened?" I finally asked. The stew filled me with warmth, the carrots a perfect softness, the meat salty and tender, and the onions and potatoes just the perfect diced size to add flavor and comfort.

"We were attacked," he said, his voice low and smoky. "The ship bore the flag of Corallure, so the king or prince–one of them–sent an assassin to kill me."

I blinked. King Halstead? Crown Prince Damien? Or Prince Elias? They wouldn't do such a thing... unless...

"Were you whaling off the shores?" I asked.

"I was on a mission from the queen," he said, his tone impatient. My heart froze at the word "queen."

He's loyal to her, I thought, and that re-emphasized the reality: He had to go as soon as possible. So how was I going to get him out of here?

Help him heal faster, I told myself. I was an herb witch, and I'd pull out all the stops for him.

He looked around, his fingers fidgeting, his jaw tightening. He kept checking his wound as if looking at it might speed up the healing.

Good. I would encourage him to get out of here as as soon as he could.

"Would you like more?" I asked, noticing Alaric had finished his bowl and was staring at it.

"I'm not going to eat all your food–" he started to say when I took it from him. Our fingers brushed and I noticed how cold his hands were. That was not a good sign.

"I cooked plenty," I said, hurrying to the kitchen, my cheeks heating as his gaze followed me. "Besides," I added. "I'd rather overfeed you then stitch you up again."

When I returned, the huntsman leaned against the back of the settee, his face pale, like even eating itself wore him out. How old was he? I recalled him being very young. Was it three years older than myself?

Twenty-five. That sounded and looked about right for him.

"I will pay you back a hundredfold–" he said as I sat on the settee to gently hand him the bowl.

But I snapped back first. "I don't want your blood money, whaler."

The words were out before I could stop them, sharp as a foraging knife.

Silence fell between us.

He blinked, stunned. Not angry. Just... surprised. As if no one had ever spoken to him like that. My pulse raced, my fingers shaking as I handed him his bowl.

But I didn't take my words back.

I'd spent years holding my tongue, shrinking myself to keep the peace. I didn't know what came over me now. Maybe it was the exhaustion, the fear, or that I'd just done everything in my power to save this man's life... and perhaps, in tending him, a dangerous feeling brewed inside.

Care.

He looked down at the bowl, then back at me, quiet now. Like a tide pulling back after a storm.

"Alright," he finally said.

I exhaled, tension leaving my shoulders like smoke. "I didn't mean to—"

"No, you did. And you should've." His voice was rasped, softened. "I've hurt people. I know what I am."

Something flickered in his expression. Regret, maybe? Or just the ghost of it.

Then, before I could turn away, he spoke.

"By the way..." He cleared his throat. "Thank you. For saving my life."

I stilled.

The words were unexpected. Gentle. Real.

I swallowed hard. Nobody had ever... *appreciated* me.

"You're welcome," I whispered.

I kept my head turned so I could see him in my peripherals. And, for a moment, we simply sat in the room's hush. The wind blew outside, the hearth crackled, the steam rose from the bowls. It wasn't peace, exactly, but something like it. A small, shared quiet.

I tucked a loose strand of hair behind my ear, his gaze following the motion.

I've hurt people. I know what I am. His voice rang in my mind.

Perhaps I'm being too unkind, I thought. Maybe, just maybe, there was more to Alaric than the beast persona he wore. Something in me still wanted to believe in second chances, even if I believed *I* could never receive such a merciful thing.

CHAPTER FIVE

ALARIC

The days bled together.

Sleep. Wake. Eat. Sleep again.

My body refused to cooperate, and that alone was enough to make me irritable. I hated weakness. Hated the way my limbs trembled when I tried to sit up too long. Hated the distant throb of pain in my side that reminded me I was still alive, but not by much.

She didn't hover, which surprised me. The girl—who, frustratingly, would not tell me her name–moved around the cottage quietly, like wind threading through the fibers of the sail. She tended the herbs hanging from the beams, stirred the pot without a word, wiped my brow when a fever broke, then left me to my silence.

That silence unnerved me.

No one in my world was ever quiet. They shouted orders, barked commands, spilled blood while laughing or crying. But she had a stillness about her, a kind of grounded calm that filled the room without demanding anything.

And maybe that's what caught me off guard. Not her

beauty, though she had it in spades. Warm brown eyes, sun-kissed skin, hair like black water. But her presence...

Unshaken. Even now, with a wounded stranger in her home.

She didn't fear me. Not quite.

Furthermore, she held herself like a polished princess. There was nothing rough or sharp about her.

Each footstep was graceful.

Each word was spoken clearly and gently.

She never raised her voice, and kept her chin up.

That behavior strangely reminded me of Sereth, but in a whole other way.

I shifted beneath the blanket, trying not to grimace. The wound tugged with every breath. She'd stitched me up like a sailor patching torn sails. Deft and fast, not pretty, but it'd hold.

The door creaked. I turned my head slowly to find her bringing in some herbs. She noticed my empty bowl and picked it up.

"Round four?" I rasped, voice rough as driftwood.

She offered a faint smile. "It's actually round five, but who's counting?"

My mouth twitched. Not quite a smile, but close. How long had I been here, eating her home cooked meals that made my heart twist with nostalgia?

She set the bowl beside me and turned to grab a cloth, probably to cool my forehead again. I cleared my throat.

"My men."

She paused, glanced at me. "Yes?"

"My crew. They'll think I'm dead by now. Or captured." I forced myself upright, teeth clenched against the pain. "I need to send word."

"I can send a message," she said, gently but firm. "But you need to rest."

"If they think I am in danger..."

"I'll tell them you're alive. Just healing, but safe. And that you should stay put."

I studied her. "You don't know them. They won't take your word."

"Then you can write the message yourself." She offered a scrap of parchment and a quill from the nearby mantel. "I'll make sure it's delivered."

Ginger thought of everything.

I took the items from her hand, foreign to the way just the brush of her fingers tickled my heart.

I dipped the quill into the ink, then paused.

In simplicity, my men would recognize my voice.

Safe. Healing. Hold position.

I signed my name and handed it back.

She took it without question, folding it carefully. "Who should I give it to?"

"Destin. My cousin. First mate."

She nodded, already turning toward the door.

"Ginger," I said before I could stop myself.

She turned back. "Yes?"

I didn't know what I meant to say. "Thank you" felt too small. "I owe you my life" felt too large.

So instead, I made a playful guess. "Is your name Anne?"

She tipped her head, as if amused. "Not close." Perhaps we could make a game of this to pass the time.

"Rain?"

The corner of her lip turned up. "It should've been."

Silence, then she held up the letter. "I'll be back soon."

I wanted to say more, and in a rush of words that didn't

feel like me, I said, "I appreciate you... and all you've done for me."

A beat of silence passed between us. Then, she nodded, a trace of a smile on her face. "I'm doing what anyone else would do." It was as if she wanted to dismiss the idea that she had been helpful at all, her eyes looking past me.

She left, her skirts brushing the floor like leaves on stone.

And for the first time in a long time, I didn't mind the stillness she left behind.

"ALRIGHT, I'M GETTING UP," I said. "The sooner I walk around, the better." A groan escaped as I tried to sit up, the pain in my side flaring. I froze and cursed under my breath, to which Ginger said, "Don't."

"Sorry," I muttered, knowing that *not* cursing would take some time to get used to if I was going to be here much longer. My chest heaved with the effort to stay still, the muscles in my back and shoulder tight with strain.

The woman sat beside me in an instant, her hand at my back. The warmth ignited something in me.

"I'm fine," I said, but she braced herself to help me stand as I rested my left arm over her shoulders. She was so small compared to me, yet, at the same time, she was the perfect size.

Alaric, I warned myself.

"You're not fine," Ginger whispered. "But you will be."

I let out a short laugh, but the pain kept me from doing more than wincing. "At least I can walk."

Her gaze was sympathetic as she slowly stepped away from me. "For now. But don't push it."

And with that, she helped me to the washroom, where I

could relieve myself. I desperately wanted to bathe, but I didn't have the strength to do so, and returned to the settee, completely winded.

"You lost a lot of blood," the woman said, handing me a plate of rice and *laulau,* pork wrapped in taro leaves and cooked through. The salty aroma filled the room, and my stomach grumbled in response. As I took the plate, I couldn't help but notice she rolled up her sleeves today. And now I could see so much more.

Burn scars.

They laced up her hands, arms, disappearing under her clothes until they reached her neck. Where did she get those? How did it spread from her hands to her neck?

"It will take a few days to get back to your normal strength." She sat on the rocking chair across from me and ate her own food, her head tipped as she carefully prepared her bite. It was odd... Why didn't she just *look* at her food?

"The good news though is that your fever has broken, which means the wound is no longer infected." She motioned to my food, inviting me to eat. But I wasn't quite ready to eat, because this time, being fully conscious, I couldn't stop looking at her eyes, trying to figure her out.

Each time I thought she was meeting my eyes, she seemed to be looking... beyond me? Above me? To the side of me? It was as if our eyes never quite locked.

Is she a witch? I'd heard witches had poor eyesight. Or maybe she was just ignoring me? It seemed beyond shyness at this point because she kept turning her head to see me.

I wanted to ask, but it seemed rather... rude.

The fact I could not categorize her frustrated me. I was used to command, control, order. And she did not fit into any box.

Mother's lessons came rushing back to me. *Manners first.*

"Thank you for helping me," I said, and I meant it.

The salve she'd put on my wound before dinner eased the pain in my side, and I was able to relax. Just a little. It had a cooling effect and smelled like mint and aloe.

"This salve... did you make it?"

"I did." She smiled, as if pleased with herself, suddenly rattling off herbs and natural remedies she'd used to make it. She finished with, "It also contains a good amount of cleansing alcohol in it to disinfect the wound."

I eyed her suspiciously.

Her vast knowledge only confirmed what I'd figured out. "Are you a witch?"

Her face paled, and she opened her mouth twice to speak. And though she was looking at me, it seemed she wasn't looking *directly* at me.

There was no doubt in my mind now. I frowned. "Don't put any spells on me–"

"I don't cast spells," she snapped. "And if you want to label me as a *witch,* then you should label me correctly as an *herb witch.*"

I raised an eyebrow. "Herb witch. Witch. What difference does it make?"

"Plenty of difference." The conversation obviously upset her.

She took her meal to finish in the kitchen alone. I sat back, chewing over her words. Maybe I'd struck a nerve... or maybe she simply didn't like being accused of her true identity. Either way, the tension in the room lingered when she returned to collect my bowl.

I cleared my throat, the edge of our argument still

prickling at me, and opted for a change of subject. "Would I be able to bathe?"

"Not in the tub, especially with your wound still not healed," she said. The tension in her expression softened, as if she'd already forgotten what she was angry at me for.

That look drove me crazy. Nobody should look at me like that, and yet...

I was getting used to it. Getting used to her.

Get cleaned up, I reprimanded myself. A good bath would make me feel more like myself, not the shell of a man who owned the wealthiest and most powerful whaling business in the Tempest Seas.

Saltwater, blood, and debris still soiled my hair. Sweat and healing cuts and scrapes made every inch of my skin feel sticky. Though we focused on the large gash, we could give a little more attention to the other wounds. A good bath would get everything off.

But Ginger was right. It would be a bad idea to submerge my wound in water.

"I have an idea," the witch said, and disappeared before I could say a word. When she returned, she had prepared a large clay bowl with warm water, steam still rising from it. She knelt beside me and began dabbing the cloth on my chest.

I grit my teeth, knowing I should *not* be reacting to her touch the way I was. This was ridiculous, yet it felt so... good. I reasoned it felt good because I was finally beginning to feel clean again.

I'm not clean, I thought and frowned to myself.

When she moved to my back, her fingers skimmed my scars. "What happened here?" she murmured, and I knew which scar she referred to, but I closed my eyes to try to dispel the memory.

"Huntsmen don't live soft lives."

Why were her fingers still touching it? I turned, though it caused my teeth to grit, before I caught her wrist and asked, "Enjoying yourself, witch?"

Her eyes widened, her cheeks blossoming with color as she pulled her hand away, breaking the moment. "Just trying to keep you alive, huntsman."

And my heart never felt so alive. This was ridiculous.

She worked in silence for a long while before trying to figure out how to clean my hair. We decided that if I could prop myself up on my elbows, she'd be able to wash my hair in the clay bowl. Part of me wanted to just forget it, but the other part desperately wanted the grime out of my hair. I'd feel more presentable, more like myself than a half-alive corpse.

"Your whalebone necklace is on the mantle," she said quietly, as if she'd been deep in thought. And it bothered me that she had probably been deep in thought about *me.*

Her fingers brushed through my hair, sometimes touching my forehead. She had to change the water out twice because my hair was so dirty, a thought that made me feel more embarrassed than it should.

"It was from the first whale I killed," I said, and when she didn't press me any further, I decided to not share anymore. But, after a moment, she asked, "Did it scare you?"

"What?"

"Killing the whale?"

I pursed my lips. "I was mostly afraid I'd miss or not kill it, and the thing would have the harpoon stuck in it, living a miserable life in pain..."

More silence. "You've killed so many of them." It sounded as if she spoke more to herself than to me.

"I don't glorify it," I said. "I've killed them–many times. They've fed my crew. Built my fleet. Given me power and independence any man would dream of."

"But they're sacred," she said. "Living, breathing spirits. What did they do to deserve the torture and murder you've done to them?"

So she was one of those people. Most saw whalers as just sailors, a cog in the great wheel of ocean trade. But some saw us as killers. They preached about the "rights" of whales, as if beasts could understand rights. To them, we were the lowest of the low.

Normally, I'd roll my eyes and let their words wash off like seawater. But I found myself saying, "I haven't raised a harpoon in years. My men do all that now."

"You haven't raised a harpoon," she said, and left the rest in the air between us: *But you haven't walked away, either.*

"I'm not leaving the whaling business."

She didn't argue. Just finished drying my hair, the towel catching gently at the ends before her fingers combed through it. My heart lurched. It was foreign, unwelcome. I braced against it like I would a storm.

What in the briny seas was that feeling?

"We're from two different worlds," she said, standing. And I knew what she meant: when I healed, I'd go my way, and she'd go hers.

Yet the thought needled at me. And the fact it bothered me—that leaving her bothered me—was even more irritating.

BY THE SECOND WEEK, I could sit up long enough to pretend I wasn't completely useless.

I had attempted to bathe in the washroom but I was too weak. Ginger gave me towels to wipe my body, but I truly just needed a good bath.

I felt like a beached whale: a mass of deadweight that didn't move and smelled like rot. How the girl could stand to be around me was truly a mystery.

The sun filtered through the jealousie windows like gold dust, and a soft breeze stirred the scent of ginger and salt through the little cottage. I'd grown used to the rhythm of this place: simple meals, soft-footed care, and the quiet hum of her voice as she moved about. It was maddening, in a way. Gentle. Easy. Dangerous.

Ginger entered the room holding a woven basket and a stack of books against her hip. She gave me a look–in her strange head-turned way–that was both kind and bossy.

"You should come sit outside," she said, tipping her chin toward the little patch of shade just beyond the cottage. "Under the coconut fronds. The sun will do you good."

"I don't need the sun," I muttered, shifting my sore body against the cushions. "I need to be back on my feet."

She rolled her eyes. "One step at a time, whaler. You don't have to do anything once we're outside. Just relax and breathe." Her gaze softened. "Please."

I let her help me outside, her small shoulders under my massive arm.

The palm leaves rustled against each other and the air smelled of salt and sea.

The ocean shimmered in the distance and whales breached.

Ginger set a quilt on the ground, laid out a few books, and arranged a couple of pillows like she had all the time in the world.

When I didn't reach for any of the books, she offered one.

"No thanks." I lied down and stared at the leaves above.

It was just a short walk, I thought in frustration.

But I was panting, breathless, like I'd run for miles.

Ginger lied down next to me, our shoulders touching, and read her book. Her face was slightly turned towards me, her eyes on the coconut trees to the side. Was that how she read?

I glanced sideways, unintentionally reading the words on the page. "What is this?" I asked.

"A story from the old island kingdoms," she said, running her fingers gently along the page. "About a fisherman who fell in love with a princess."

"That sounds ridiculous," I grunted.

She ignored me. "Want me to read it out loud?"

I didn't answer. She looked at me–though her eyes looked beyond mine. Her face was so close to mine. Her vanilla scent enveloped me and I had to look up at the palm leaves to pretend that she didn't affect me.

After a moment, I said, "Sure."

Don't know why I said sure.

Maybe I just needed something... A distraction from her sweet scent. Her gentle presence.

She read aloud, her voice smooth and slow, like waves lapping a canoe.

And blast it if I didn't start to enjoy it.

Her voice wove between the lines. Warm, expressive, patient. I didn't understand why the fisherman didn't just marry a commoner, but there was something strangely captivating about the story. And then somehow my attention moved from the trees above to Ginger.

I was half-listening to the story, half-watching the sunlight catch in her long dark hair.

I didn't know how long we stayed like that. The words washed over me, unhurried, and I closed my eyes.

Then I heard the crunch of boots on the path.

I sat up too fast and winced. Ginger reached out to steady me, but I waved her off, already recognizing the voices.

"Captain?" came Destin's familiar, somber voice.

I turned to see him and Thatcher emerge from the trees, looking like they'd just come home from battle. Mud on their boots, sweat streaking their faces, scars and bruises lining their skin, and relief shining in their eyes when they saw me.

"Took you long enough," I said, voice gruff with emotion I didn't want to show. I was glad to see them alive, but also slightly bitter, though I didn't know why.

"You're alive," Thatcher said, then added, "And reading fairy tales." A grin spread across his face as he looked from me to the witch, as if seeing us *together* made him happier than just seeing me. "Thought we'd lost you for good."

I didn't even bother with a comeback. Just nodded as they both clapped my hands. Destin hugged me but quickly pulled back as I grimaced.

Malia brushed coconut fronds from her dark skirt, her head turned as she eyed them. Destin gave her a slight bow. "Miss."

She nodded back.

"Where are the twins?" I asked, my voice tightening. "How many did we lose? Why did the Corallure crown attack us? Is the Crimson Wake gone?"

Destin shook his head and held up his palm. "Everything's alright, captain. We lost four men."

I grimaced. Four men. Still too many men.

"The rest are recovering at the inn right now. And, from what we've been told by the guards at the port... it wasn't Corallure that attacked us."

"They had the coat of arms," I snapped but Destin shook his head.

"It wasn't them, Captain. We received word that the king's ships are going to keep an eye out for this mystery ship that attacked. The messenger got a bit touchy when we blamed them, and said we're lucky to be alive. The king has asked for shipbuilders to the port to help fix the Crimson Wake—they want us out of here. If we're lucky, we should sail out of here soon. Nearly all three thousand barrels of oil intact."

At the mention of the barrels, Ginger visibly tensed.

This conversation seemed so out of place, maybe even inappropriate and callous around someone as soft as Ginger.

"And the twins?" I asked again.

"They're gone." Destin pursed his lips. That hit like a blow to the ribs. It was my one promise to Sereth...

Thatcher folded his arms and shrugged. "Soon as we got to shore, they took off into the woods."

Ginger's eyes widened and she watched as Destin handed me the sealed note from Sereth. "Figured you should hold onto that."

"You need to find them," I said.

"Already sent some men out to investigate," my first mate quickly responded.

Thatcher, always the one to joke when it wasn't the time for it, said, "They were probably just scared of you... or Sereth, like everyone else."

I clenched my jaw and slipped the note into my shirt pocket without a word.

Ginger was quiet beside me. She played with a strand of hair at the mention of Sereth.

Destin and Thatcher exchanged a glance, but said nothing.

"We'll keep searching for the twins," Thatcher said, standing. "But we wanted to make sure you weren't, you know, dead."

"Thanks," I muttered.

Destin glanced at Ginger, then Thatcher, then me. "Is there anything else you need, captain?"

"Keep investigating what ship attacked us," I said. "I want to hold them responsible for the deaths of my men."

They nodded.

Destin asked, "Are you planning to rejoin the crew? We can help you walk back."

And then it hit me. *When* could I? I wasn't in a position to ride a horse, or to walk to the port. From what Ginger said, it was a good mile or two...

Could I make it that far right now?

Not yet.

Back at the inn, I'd probably have the town doctor come in and check on me.

He'd be cold. Calculated.

We'd eat food provided by the inn.

But I couldn't leave yet.

Shouldn't overdo it when I was healing at a steady pace.

I looked at Ginger and she pursed her lips. It was an awkward moment.

Part of me wanted to go, to be reunited with my crew and figure things out.

And the other part knew I was not yet recovered to take such a journey.

“I don’t want to impose. I’ve been here long enough–” I started to say when Ginger placed her hand on mine.

It caused a million foreign feelings inside of me. And self consciousness too. I didn’t want my men to see me like this.

But how could I get angry at her?

“You should probably wait a few more days–even a week or so,” she said, adding, “And you are welcome to stay here.”

I nodded and turned to my men.

Thatcher grinned. “Don’t get too comfortable here, Captain. You're starting to go soft.”

Was I?

I raised a brow. “Get back out there before I throw something.”

They left with a salute and a bit more spring in their step.

It was good to see each other. To know that we’d all survived.

We had a long road ahead, but at least we were alive.

Once they were gone, Ginger looked at me. I met her gaze. Neither of us said anything for a long while. The wind rustled through the trees again. The waves broke in the distance.

Finally, I leaned back again. Stared at the palm trees.

She lay down beside me.

Silent.

“Your cousin... did you grow up together?” she asked.

I watched the light filtering through the fronds. “Yes. Started out on a different whaling ship, then he jumped on when I started my own business.”

"How did you get the money for a ship?"

"Leased it, then paid it off quickly with the whale oil."

Those had been very rough times. Rough beginnings.

"I didn't come from wealth or luxury," I said. "You'd understand, I'm sure."

Didn't mean for it to be offensive, but, based on the run-down cottage, Ginger didn't seem like much of a wealthy person either.

More silence. Then, softly, "I used to have a nanny," she said. "And a tutor... which is how I learned to read."

Frowning, I looked at her.

This truth revealed something: she hadn't grown up poor. I figured she taught herself to read.

But now that I thought of it...

She did seem quite educated. Like she *had* read a lot of books.

On herbs and plants, specifically.

"How'd you end up out here?" I asked. Had she grown up in Corallure in a wealthy family? Why wasn't she married off to a wealthy man, then? Or reveling in the things that high society did?

"Once my stepsister came into the picture, I was no longer needed."

Stepsister?

"Anyway." She cleared her throat, fingers idly tracing the edge of the book. "Life's like a wild garden—you think you've learned every leaf and root, and then a new bloom rises from the soil, one you've never seen before. Just when you think you know it all, you find out how much you never really did."

She was right.

Because I was in the thick of it right now.

Just when I thought I knew enough about people, there was this young woman before me.

A mystery–a beautiful mystery.

Someone I wanted to figure out.

Even if I knew anything between us was forbidden, maybe even wrong and unnatural.

We were so different. Too different.

And yet... I brushed my hand against hers. Her skin was soft. Her hand small compared to mine.

The touch sent warmth through my entire body.

Her breath hitched.

"Mind reading me the rest of the story?" I asked.

I had too many things to worry about: the twins, figuring out who ambushed us, making sure the ship-builders did a good job repairing the Crimson Wake, and figuring out her... Ginger.

But it could all wait for a moment longer.

She smiled softly and opened the book.

CHAPTER SIX
MALIA

The days wore on forever. It was like waiting for herbs to dry.

One evening, after Alaric excused himself, I paused, watching him move slow but stubborn as ever to the other room. Now the sound of water splashing echoed faintly from the washroom.

The sky had dimmed. What was once golden sunlight had cooled to a dull gray, and shadows stretched long across the cottage floor. I glanced at the open shutters. Thick clouds crept across the sky like bruises.

The ocean, visible in slivers through the palms, was no longer blue. It was steel.

I sliced chunks of taro and put them into boiling water in silence, listening to the air hush outside, the way the world seemed to hold its breath before the rain broke loose. In the hearth, the fire hissed as wind slipped through the cracks of the window frame. The scent of smoke and sea salt curled around me.

A low rumble rolled across the distant sky. Thunder.

Why was I feeling anxious? Everything was alright.

Alaric was healing well.

Each day a little more strength seemed to return to him.

He'd be out of here in just a few more days if we kept this up.

And then it hit me.

It wasn't just the storm coming in. It was the feeling in my chest. That strange, unshakable knowing. Like something was shifting.

A wind howled outside and I shivered as the rainstorm picked up, battering the windows with wet, salty air.

It was at that moment, when I was deep in thought, clumsily moving about the kitchen as I normally did, that the cottage door slammed open. I was so startled, a scream didn't even escape my lips as a man burst inside, soaked through, his blade drawn.

He was tall and slender, but anyone could tell that his eyes glistened with hatred. With the knife still in hand, my breath hitched.

"Where is he?" the intruder growled, eyes fixed on me as he stepped forward, mud dragging into my home. "I need proof that he's dead."

Proof that he's dead? I gaped, frozen in fear. The man moved closer, and that's when my brain kicked in.

"What are you talking about?" I asked. Alaric was still in the washroom, and I hoped he stayed there until I got this man to leave. But the man grabbed my arms, forcing the cutting knife to the floor.

And that's when panic settled in.

"Those villagers told me he was here."

Those villagers! Perhaps Alaric's crew let it slip, or others somehow found out. Gossip spread like wildfire around here. "You're the witch aren't you? Did you curse him? Eat him? *Where* is he?"

I swallowed hard. This had to be the assassin who tried to kill Alaric... but he also looked... strangely familiar.

Those eyes... filled with... remorse. Had we met before?

"Whoever you're looking for is not–"

The man pushed me to the wall, and my head hit it so hard, everything turned white for a moment.

"You're hiding him! If you don't tell me where he is, you will regret it witch!"

And that was when someone tore him away from me.

"Don't touch her."

One arm was clutched across his side, the fresh bandages protecting his wound. But his other hand grabbed the back of the assassin's collar and yanked, slamming the man off balance and into the wall. A bowl shattered on the floor. Alaric staggered, panting hard, gripping the table by the entrance for support.

"Run!" he barked at me.

But I couldn't leave him. I watched in horror.

The assassin twisted, aiming for Alaric's ribs, where he was already wounded. Alaric saw it too. His movements weren't quick. But they were smart. He kicked out the assassin's knee... hard. The man went down with a thud. The knife scraped across the wood floor.

Alaric didn't go for it.

Instead, he used his weight, leaning his body against the attacker's, dragging him down. "Give me the blade," he said, voice hoarse. I scrambled, grabbed it, and tossed it toward him.

He caught it in one hand, and the moment the assassin reached up, Alaric slammed the hilt into the man's temple. Once. Twice.

"Stop!" I exclaimed. One more hit and he'd kill the man.

"I'll kill you," Alaric growled, his tone raw. "I should kill you."

My feet moved of their own accord and I placed my hand on Alaric's arm. There was no way I could pry his fingers off the knife, or even try to move his arm away.

I had to use my voice.

"Please," I said. "Please let him go–"

"He would've killed you. Or me. Or both of us." Alaric didn't look at me. His eyes were locked on the man beneath him. The whaler seethed with fury.

"Alaric." My voice was firm, but gentle. "This isn't right. This isn't who you are." Who was I to say such a thing? He was a stranger to me, yet... somehow, deep inside, I knew there had to be some good. Even though I despised whalers, and should despise Alaric out of them all, I knew there was more to him.

There was more to everyone, except me, I supposed.

The man's eyes were wide, darting between myself and Alaric. My hand slid down to the whaler's wrist, my fingers curling around his. "Let him go."

Alaric closed his eyes, just for a moment. Then he growled. "Who do you work for?"

"Corallure—"

"You're lying and you know it. The king has no such assassin ships. *Who do you work for?*"

Fear pooled in the man's eyes. "I swore I'd never say."

"Then better to be silent," Alaric threatened, moving the blade to the man's neck.

"Alaric," I warned. He shoved the assassin. "Get out," he said. "Don't ever show your face again or I *will* kill you next time." And just like that, the man scrambled out into the rain, leaving us in a thick tension.

Silence fell. The only sound left was Alaric's ragged

breathing, the soft crackle of the fire, and the taro chunks still bubbling on the hearth as if nothing had happened.

I knelt beside him, hands trembling, reaching for his side. Blood. Too much blood. "Alaric, you're hurt—"

He didn't look at me. Just stared down at the floor, jaw tight, eyes blazing with something I couldn't name.

"Now you know," he murmured. "No one touches you."

Then he slumped forward. My heart raced.

Help him, Malia!

For the amount of pain he must've been experiencing, he kept his emotions in check. He didn't scream or cry. He didn't even moan. Instead, he grit his teeth, his jaw set, his fists curled. I quickly helped him up.

"We have to stitch it back up," I said, and he allowed me to guide him back to the settee. If we didn't contain his wound, he might lose too much blood and then... well...

Don't think like that, I told myself, both annoyed and amused that I cared so much.

I shuddered as I grabbed my needle and thread. "Who was that?" I asked after a moment of silence.

Alaric watched me, his eyes going between my face and the needle. His body was tense, but I couldn't blame him. He hadn't relaxed from the adrenaline-packed encounter. My own fingers were slightly shaking, and it took all my concentration to see where the stitches had burst.

"He was the assassin from the ship. The ship bore Corallure's coat of arms." He grimaced as I worked. I was not one to get squeamish at the sight of blood or wounds, but, at this rate that the whaler was going, I might just start.

I didn't reply to him, but, instead, quietly said, "*Please* don't do that again–"

"And let him hurt you?"

I glanced at him, and, for a moment, color blossomed in his cheeks, something that seemed impossible for a man as rough as this whaler.

I pursed my lips, a weird sensation spreading through me. It was warm, like sipping steaming hibiscus tea on a cold night.

"Thank you." My voice was quiet, and the whaler gave me one final look before taking a breath and relaxing on his back, his eyes closing in exhaustion.

After placing a clean bandage over his wound, I sat back and let out a slow breath. This was intense—every part of it. Housing a man who could kill without hesitation. I knew he was dangerous but now... I shuddered. Alaric could inflict damage on anyone in his path. Including me.

Except he wouldn't.

My gaze lingered on his face, relaxed in sleep, his breathing even. My heart betrayed me with a small, aching tug.

He had saved my life. Stepped between me and danger without a second thought. Not because he had to—at least, I didn't think so—but because he didn't want me hurt. I couldn't remember the last time someone had done that for me.

Somewhere between the fear and the mistrust, I'd begun to care whether he lived. And that unsettled me more than any wound or whispered threat.

I shook my head, sealing the thought away. I would keep him alive. I would see him healed. But he could never know who I really was.

Because if he learns the truth of my past, he'll see me for what I truly am.

The monster. The witch.

CHAPTER SEVEN
ALARIC

I was in and out of consciousness, and each time I woke, the woman would notice and tend to me. The pain in my side hurt more than being gored by a harpoon: deep, hot, and lingering.

But I wasn't about to soften now. Not with her near. Not when the weight of what had happened clung to me like wet, sea-drenched clothes.

When I finally woke to full consciousness, the memories came rushing in like a rising tide:

The ambush.

The flash of steel.

The assassin showing up here, in this woman's home—her sacred space.

How could he? It was as if he violated a place and a woman I was just beginning to learn about...

The young woman. I saved her life, even when she never asked it of me.

The way she touched my hand, like I was something worth saving, and whispered that I wasn't the kind of man to kill another.

She believed that.

Even when I didn't.

I've killed men before. Maybe not intentionally, but I'd run my men ragged. I branded them, scarred them, yelled at them, threatened them...

My throat was dry, and every breath felt like fire. I turned my head toward the rocking chair where she usually sat, but it was empty.

Though, I knew she'd been watching over me. Tending me.

Still here.

If only she knew who I really was. I blinked and looked around. It had to be midday, with an island breeze sweeping through the windows. Outside, birds chirped and coconut fronds brushed against each other. Ocean waves rolled in the distance.

I was getting used to this peaceful atmosphere.

I probably shouldn't.

A woman's voice hummed and the witch came inside, carrying a basket of herbs. I watched as she worked, laying out dried herbs on the counter, her head always turned–it seemed–to look at anything but what she actually did with her hands. Her long black hair fell behind her, almost reaching her bottom. She was petite, but not lacking feminine qualities.

Ginger. The way she tended to me was gentle, and each time I woke up to see her face, I knew I was safe. I could rest.

Why won't she tell me her name? And why did it nag at me that after all this time she still kept it to herself?

She pulled apart some dried lavender when her face turned slightly. "Are you awake?" she asked, but she wasn't exactly looking at me.

I tried to sit up, but she was immediately at my side. "Gently. I need to rebandage this."

"I need to walk," I said, and she nodded.

"You will. Just let me take care of this first." And then she was there, removing the bandage and moving close to me. Much too close.

"It's fine," I said, though when I dared to look at it, my fingers twitched. The wound looked bad. The entire area was purple and green around the thick red line. It was mottled-looking, with the skin looking stretched and worn.

And though it hurt, I suddenly became way too aware of the woman's touch.

"It's not fine," she said. "Relax."

But I couldn't relax, not when she pressed her hand on my chest, forcing me to lie back down. I tensed as she leaned in, her fingers brushing my skin as she worked, her hair touching my bare shoulder.

I grit my teeth... not because of the pain, but because I could feel the warmth of her breath on my collarbone. She smelled like vanilla and plumerias, a scent both refreshing and warm.

A scent I should not be thinking about.

"You're too tense," she said again, her fingers touching the wound as she cleaned up dry blood and placed her salve on it.

"Maybe because I have a woman fussing over me," I said, and I meant it. I was not used to being cared for like this, to being *touched* at all.

Much to my surprise, her expression softened and the corner of her lip turned up. "Maybe if the huntsman wasn't so reckless, he wouldn't need fussing over."

At this, I smirked. "Careful, Ginger. You're starting to sound like you care."

With those words, crimson colored her cheeks. "I don't–" she started to say, then shook her head, placed a fresh bandage on my wound, then left to clean her hands. But there was an undeniable tension in the air, one that filled me with something I'd never felt before.

I took a little breath, hoping it would dispel whatever was there, but it wouldn't go away, much to my chagrin.

CHAPTER EIGHT
MALIA

This man was just another whaler, and I silently resented him for it. Perhaps when he saved my life, I thought he might be a good man after all. Perhaps there was someone, under all that muscle and brute strength, who had a heart.

But he was like the others. He lived off killing whales. He thrived off of it. As I prepared another clay bowl of warm water to wash his wounds, I couldn't help but roll my eyes at the irony of the situation. A girl who loved the whales, saving a man who killed them.

I looked out to sea, said a silent prayer asking for patience, then approached Alaric. He sat at the edge of the couch, looking much better today than the past few days. His color had returned, and he was moving around a lot more. But his wounds still needed tending, and, while he said I didn't need to do it, I wanted to.

Because the sooner he was better, the sooner he'd leave.

I bent down in front of him, gently taking the bandages off. I dabbed the wound on his forehead, gently. But silently, I felt flustered. He was so close, I could feel his warmth, a sensation I was not used to. I couldn't recall the last time I'd ever been close to someone, or anyone.

Perhaps when I was a baby, my mother might have held me close. But, since my youth, I couldn't recall any memories of hugging anyone, or feeling anyone's warmth, a thought that disturbed me more than I expected.

Alaric was unusually quiet, and when I used my peripherals to see what he might be looking at, he was gazing directly at my eyes, studying me. My cheeks heated as self-consciousness flooded in.

Was he going to ask about my eyes? I knew, sooner or later, he might.

A gentle breeze wafted through the room, carrying the scent of ginger snaps and banana bread. I'd been hard at work that morning baking for the farmer's market the next day. I hadn't let Noni know last time if I'd do it again, so I hoped to go out for a walk that night and deliver them to her.

Ginger. Witch. Now he had two names for me. At least he didn't know my real name. The whaler suddenly did something I was not expecting–maybe he wasn't even expecting it. He gently tucked my hair behind my ear. The move was so gentle, so unexpected, my heart pounded in my chest.

But before he or I could say or do something, someone knocked on the door.

"Malia!" And then the door opened, Noni bursting in. It all happened so quickly. I was startled, thinking it might be the assassin at my doorstep, and, in my panic, I jerked back. My foot caught the edge of the clay bowl and I would've fallen backward had Alaric not grabbed my hands.

And suddenly I fell right into him, my arms splayed

across his bare chest. He instinctively caught me, one hand around my waist and the other bracing me against him.

For a moment, the whole world was dead silent. My eyes were wide, with color creeping up my neck, tingling my ears and burning my cheeks. Alaric still held me, his lips near my ear.

And Noni gasped. "Malia! Oh my! I will come back later–"

"Noni!" I scrambled to stand. "Wait! Wait, I was just helping him–"

The woman raised an eyebrow, as though she were amused. "Yes, I can see that."

And meanwhile, Alaric sat there, a smirk on his face, like he thought this exchange was rather funny. "This isn't the worst thing that's happened to me lately," he said, and Noni laughed.

"I'll be back, Malia!"

"No, *wait!*" I *had* to explain myself! I could not bear the thought of Noni believing I was some promiscuous girl caught with a whaler. I'd endured enough, and this would not be another mark on my already scorned record. I rushed out after her, spilling out the events of the last few weeks.

"He *needs* to get better," I said. "I need him to leave."

"Why? Because you're catching feelings?" Noni winked. "He's one to look at–"

"Noni!" I gasped. "No, listen. Once he's better, he'll be gone. There is absolutely nothing between us. You know how I feel about whalers."

Noni softened, and my shoulders relaxed. She believed me. "Yes, I know you love the whales. We all do." She nodded and gently patted my shoulder. "Why don't you get those baked goods and I'll be on my way? We'll chat more about this another day."

Whew. I nodded, "Thank you, Noni." She believed me! Thank goodness, because that was wildly embarrassing! And the emotions coursing through my body didn't help. I ignored Alaric, grabbed the goods from the kitchen, and gave them to Noni, thanking her for selling them at the market.

And then she was gone, leaving me standing at the front of my cottage. My stomach twisted.

Now I had to deal with him again.

When I re-entered the cottage, I found Alaric changing the bandages on his arm. "Well that was eventful," he said, and my blush deepened.

"You should've let me fall."

"I'm not going to let you fall." He gave me a look. "I'm more of a gentleman than that."

A man who kills whales? I rolled my eyes. *Some gentleman.*

I squeezed the cloth from the bowl and began tending the wound on his back. A tense, awkward silence stretched between us as I thought about his words.

I'm not going to let you fall. Was I imagining it, or did it seem there was some underlying message?

I'm reading too much into his words, I told myself.

"This one," I said, finally breaking the silence as my fingertips hovered over the big white scar. "It wasn't from the shipwreck, right?"

The whaler exhaled slowly, the muscles in his back and arms sinking, as if something weighed them down. "No."

I didn't speak, letting him choose whether or not he wanted to share. After a moment, Alaric finally answered. "A harpoon. Years ago."

Ouch. A harpoon did this? My fingers traced the scar and Alaric stiffened. "Does it still hurt?" I asked.

He hesitated, then answered. "Not in the way you

mean." That's when he turned and looked at me. I wished he knew I was meeting his eyes, because, for a moment, his eyebrows furrowed, as if he thought I was avoiding him.

I nodded though, a deep and unspoken connection between us. The scars were so much more. "I know that kind of hurt," I said, then absentmindedly touched the burn marks on my neck, wondering if he had noticed those and the burn marks on my arms and hands.

Alaric's jaw tightened, as if he wanted to ask more, to know more. But, as I did before in giving him a choice, he let me choose to share or not too.

I said nothing. I couldn't. If I told him how I got the burn marks, he'd know who I was. But there was something so simple and kind about his gesture of letting me choose that warmed my heart. It seemed everyone was always trying to pry into my life or make assumptions about it. Yet, here he was, not forcing me to do anything, not forcing me to speak, but just being present in the silence, a silence that spoke volumes.

I cleared my throat and quickly returned to tending his wound. But for the rest of the evening, every one of his gestures did not go unnoticed: he took his time eating, as if savoring every bite. He said please and thank you, and didn't complain once about his wounds, the ill-fitting clothes, or even the settee that looked too small for a man his size. And, throughout all of it, he watched me too. But, unlike others who had watched me throughout my life, he seemed genuinely curious, and that terrified me.

Moonlight poured through my bedroom window as I tossed and turned. Why couldn't I sleep? I was exhausted. Tending to Alaric all day, plus taking care of my daily chores and tasks of cooking, baking, keeping house, and caring for my garden had worn me out. Yet I couldn't stop thinking about how *nice* it felt when I fell into Alaric's arms.

Stop, Malia! I was being ridiculous. I would *never* fall for a whaler, a huntsman who murdered innocent creatures and spent their days in riotous living at the ports. Alaric was no different, and I was probably fighting feelings of attraction.

It's natural, I told myself, but couldn't kick the feeling that there was something more. And then it hit me like bitterroot spoiling a warm tea. *I'm starting to care for him.* Memories resurfaced, of when I cared for others: a family member, two lost children...

And what happens when I start caring for people? I shuddered and drew my covers close to my chin. *They turn on me.*

Right. I couldn't afford to do such a thing again. The last two times I nearly lost my life, and this time, well... I didn't think Alaric would hurt me. But maybe there was even more at risk than my life.

A groan brought my thoughts to a swift end. I gasped and sat upright. Did Alaric accidentally turn and hurt his wound?

Please don't have reopened that wound, I thought, rushing out of bed and into the living room. But he was fast asleep, his head turning back and forth as he groaned and moaned to himself.

I couldn't make out any of his words at first, but then he said, "No... *no!*" What was he witnessing in his dream? It sounded awful. I knelt by the settee and gently shook him awake.

"Alaric, wake up."

He sat up too soon and grasped his side in pain. His

breathing was hard, his body tense, and a light sheen of sweat shone on his forehead.

"Alaric?" I kept my voice soft, careful even.

He blinked, taking me in, then wiped his forehead, sat up, and let out a breath. "It's nothing. I'm sorry I woke you up." He tried leaning forward to place his elbows on his legs, but it was too much for his wound, so he sat back and placed his arm on the backrest of the settee. It was almost as if he were inviting me to sit there next to him, but I didn't move.

I still knelt there and waited, not knowing why I ached to help, why I ached to comfort him. "Was it the sea?" I finally asked.

The wind shuffled outside, and the waves in the distance filled the silence.

Alaric didn't answer, but rubbed his face and exhaled.

"Will you tell me?" I asked, daring to sit next to him. With both of us on the settee, it now seemed rather small. And, much to my surprise and delight, he nodded, staring into the dead fireplace. "When I was a boy, I watched my father drown."

My breath caught. *Drown?*

"There was nothing I could do–nothing anyone could do. He was swept away so quickly. I tried to dive in after him but my mother wouldn't let me."

"How old were you?"

"Ten."

Stab. That was too young. Too heartbreaking to watch such a scene unfold.

"I swore I'd never be that weak." His voice was rough. "That I'd take instead of being taken from."

I wanted to do something, like touch his hand or place

my hand on his arm, but it seemed too intimate. So I spoke instead. “You were just a boy.”

Alaric finally looked at me, and, in his eyes I could see the pain, the helplessness, a feeling he tried so desperately to never feel again. My heart hurt for him, and, at the same time, I felt as if I'd been invited into something. It was like watching the perfect ingredients meld together to create a healing remedy.

“I've never shared that with anyone so...” He rubbed his forehead, as if embarrassed. “I'd appreciate if you kept that between us.”

“Of course.” I leaned back against the settee and we sat in a content silence. Yet though we were quiet, there was something happening between us, something safe, something warm.

“I didn't watch my father die,” I said, “But I know what it's like to lose him. I lost my father when I was ten too.”

Alaric looked at me, and the softness in his voice made my legs weak. “I'm so sorry, Malia.”

Malia. He knew my name now, thanks to Noni barging in on us earlier. Hearing my name on his lips warmed me from the tips of my toes to the crown of my head.

I swallowed hard, my heart pattering as Alaric asked, “What happened? If you don't mind me asking...”

For some reason, I wanted to tell him everything, but I fidgeted with the sleeves of my nightshirt and was sure not to share any names. “One night he... just didn't wake up.” It happened so suddenly that the doctor said there was no way to explain it. I finally came to the conclusion that he was called to the other side early.

“That sounds...” Alaric shook his head. “Difficult. I'm so sorry.”

“I think I would've been able to cope better if my

mother hadn't remarried so soon," I said, and Alaric frowned, but he probably figured my family was destitute and mother needed a husband to take care of us.

"Was your stepfather kind?"

"I didn't get to know him well. He was indifferent to me–all of my parents were. It was as if I was invisible to them." I played with my hair. "Sometimes I wondered if I even belonged to them. It often seemed like I was an orphan that they'd been obligated to take in."

The whaler tensed. "Why would they treat you that way?"

I shrugged. "I wondered if my mother had an affair... because I don't look like my mother *or* father. My mother had soft brown hair. And father's hair was even lighter."

And then I pulled on a strand of my midnight hair. Alaric gently touched it, his fingers brushing against mine. My heart skipped a beat.

"Were you adopted?" he asked, quickly pulling his hand back, his cheeks warm.

I shrugged. "I don't think so."

"Do you have memories of your earliest childhood?"

For some reason, I appreciated Alaric exploring this with me. I'd never told anyone–because, truly, I had nobody to talk to. Maybe I was also afraid that if I did talk to someone, they might reveal that I was, indeed, an orphan, and I had no place being in the noble family I was in.

I swallowed hard. Beyond that though, the fact that Alaric cared, that he was curious... it made me feel...

Important.

And it made me want to smile, even though the smile had nothing to do with my sad history.

"My mother gave me a necklace," I said. "I can show you later. She never explained where it came from, or why, but..." I gently touched the whalebone necklace on Alaric's chest, my palm touching his shirt. I could feel his warmth. "It reminded me of this."

"Will you show it to me later?" Alaric asked.

I nodded. "I'll have to find it in my room."

The whaler shifted. We were suddenly closer, my head practically on his chest.

"I can move–" I started to say, when Alaric laughed.

"Or you can stay."

Stay. I liked hearing him say that.

I blushed now that the whaler had his arm around my shoulders, his thumb circling lazily on my shoulder as he took a breath. "So you grew up with a stepfather?"

"He died too."

At this, Alaric gave me a look. "Your mother's husbands weren't poisoned, were they?" I wasn't sure if he meant this to be a joke, or if he was serious. I answered anyway.

"No. My stepfather died from a sickness that ailed him since youth. I was left with a stepsister."

"Ah." Alaric nodded, then let his head rest back, voice quieter. "So does any of this have to do with your secrecy? Why wouldn't you tell me your name?"

I hesitated, the answer catching in my throat. "I just... don't like people knowing," I admitted. "It felt safer that way. Especially with you."

His brow lifted slightly, but there was no offense in his tone. "Because I'm a whaler?"

"Because I didn't know if I could trust you."

He was silent for a long moment, the sound of the waves filling the space between us. Then, softly, "Do you?"

I swallowed, thinking before I answered. "Yes."

His eyes narrowed, curious. "Why?"

A hundred reasons swirled in my mind, but one rose

above them all. "Because you saved my life," I said. "And because... I think there's more to you than the man you want the world to see."

Something unreadable flickered in his gaze before his lashes lowered. "It's a pretty name," he murmured, like a secret meant only for the two of us.

My cheeks warmed as his hand squeezed my arm. He closed his eyes, his features softening into sleep. I watched him for a long moment. The light was dim, and I still had to look out the corners of my eyes, but being this close, I could get more details of his face.

I liked his rough tanned skin, dark lashes, and shadowed facial hair. He looked so rogue, yet so... calm.

I relaxed. Here was this man I'd sworn to keep at arm's length, and yet I wondered how someone could be both storm and shelter in the same breath.

And I saw him... really saw him. He wasn't just the whaler bloodying the seas.

He was a boy who was terrified of weakness.

Of the sea.

Who needed to be in control, to be the most powerful man the world had ever seen.

Because his father was not.

He was too young. Too young to witness what he did.

But no girl should have to endure what I did after my father died... For the first time, I began to feel something for myself that I never had before.

Compassion. It was warm, like snuggling in a blanket after being out in the cold.

I sighed and closed my eyes, dozing off until my head rested on his chest. His arm instinctively held me closer and I couldn't recall ever sleeping as well as I did on that night.

CHAPTER NINE ALARIC

"Are you sure you're up for it?"

Her voice was gentle, but the question sliced sharper than I expected.

I turned toward her slowly, still seated at the edge of the settee where I'd been lacing up my boots. Malia stood in the doorway, sunlight crowning her like she belonged in it.

And she did. This was her world, after all. Quiet forest paths, sea wind in her hair, bundles of herbs in her arms.

"I'm fine," I said, then cleared my throat. "Just... taking my time."

She didn't press. Just nodded and turned to gather her things: her basket, a thin black shawl, fresh loaves of banana bread and gingersnaps. All the things she always carried. Things I'd grown used to seeing, smelling, hearing.

The market meant returning to my men. It meant facing the wreckage of what was left.

My crew. The ship. The life I'd been living before washing here.

I should've been eager to go.

Instead, I stared at the spot where she had just stood.

This was for the best. She was never mine to begin with. And I was never meant to stay.

But blast it, I'd gotten used to her voice in the morning. Her calm, capable hands. The way her food tasted like home and safety.

And the other night... When she woke me from my nightmare.

I couldn't stop thinking of how good it felt to hold her, to talk to her.

I'd never opened up to anyone like that, and, as far as I knew, nobody had ever opened up to me like that.

As much as I didn't want to admit it, I was starting to really care for her.

Deeply.

I rose slowly, pain flaring in my side, but not enough to keep me here. The wound had healed. Mostly. But the ache in my chest... that one hadn't.

"You coming?" she called, already a few steps down the trail, her head tipped to the side like she always did. Never quite looking at me.

I'd even gotten used to that.

I forced a breath and followed.

"Yes," I said. "Time to go."

Even if it meant saying goodbye.

THE COASTAL MARKET WAS LOUD. Colorful fabrics snapped in the wind, laughter echoed from children weaving between stalls, and the air was thick with salt, sugarcane, and the scent of roasting meat. I stood with Malia beneath the banyan trees, feeling like a ghost tethered to the wrong world.

"Are you sure you're ready?" she asked softly, the fronds

above us casting shifting shadows over her face.

No. Not in the least.

But I nodded anyway. "I need to be."

She gave a small smile, though it didn't reach her eyes. "They'll be glad to see you."

I looked at her for a long moment. This girl—this strange, stubborn, beautiful girl—had patched me back together.

And yet, somehow, she had torn me apart at the same time.

"Malia..."

She stepped back before I could finish, as if sensing that my heart was about to betray us both. "Go," she said. "Before they think you're dead and start holding ceremonies in your honor."

I huffed a laugh, and before I could stop myself, I brushed a knuckle down her arm. "Take care of yourself, witch."

She rolled her eyes, but her mouth trembled with something softer. Then, without warning, she stood on the tips of her toes and kissed my cheek.

It was so sudden. So unexpected. It sent a jolt of warmth through me. Her vanilla and flower scent enveloped me one last time. "You too, huntsman."

I wanted to grab her and kiss her, but I didn't move. Just stood there, frozen.

She smiled, her face far more beautiful than any sunrise.

And just like that, she turned and was gone.

I NEEDED TO DISTRACT MYSELF.

The first thing I did was get clothes that fit. My men

weren't at the inn, though, but the keeper showed me the room anyway. After I cut my messy, matted hair, trimmed my facial hair, bathed, and changed into clothes that fit, I felt more like myself. I felt like I could shoot a harpoon or run along the beach or take another long walk.

Washing felt like I washed away *her.*

Memories.

Feelings.

It's all behind me, I told myself.

It was back to work now.

We had twins to find. The ship to fix. The mystery assassins to bring to justice.

I ate alone before looking for my men, hoping the food would give me the boost I needed.

But it didn't taste good.

Because it's not her food.

I was going soft, and it killed me.

Keep moving, Alaric.

Every small thing left me more winded than I hoped, but I did keep moving.

I found my men near the harbor, piles of wood and supplies all around as they repaired the Crimson Wake. She looked rough, but definitely getting better.

"Captain!" My cousin embraced me, followed by another clap on the back and hug from Thatcher. Behind them stood the survivors of my crew. They looked unharmed, unscathed. The cheers of the rest of the crew startled a flock of seabirds into flight.

What a relief. It was so good to see everyone.

"We thought you were dead," Destin said.

"I thought I was too." I rubbed my freshly-shaved chin. Destin and Thatcher brought out some mugs and motioned to the other men.

"What are you doing?" My voice was harsh.

"Drinking because we survived. You ought to get an ale too," said Thatcher, but before they could burst open a keg, I stopped them.

"We have to be aware. What if those assassins come after us? You can't fight if you're drunk."

"I fight best when I'm drunk," Thatcher joked, and I gave him a look.

The crew didn't dare laugh if I didn't. I forgot they feared me, especially when Malia hadn't.

I immediately got back to business. "What news?"

Thatcher unwillingly put the mugs and keg away. Destin motioned for the men to keep working, then watched as I slumped onto a crate. I felt every mile I'd walked. Destin knelt beside me, his hand steadying my shoulder without a word. For a heartbeat, it was like the old days, when the world was narrowed to the creak of timbers and the trust between us.

A flicker of memory: Destin pressing a flask into my hand on a cold night after the hunt went wrong. Thatcher standing guard over me in that cramped port cell when the magistrate swore I'd hang. Storms, blood, betrayals... and still, they'd been there. Still, they called me Captain.

Destin's voice broke the silence. "You look like death, cousin. But you made it back."

I nodded, then looked up at him. "Thanks for keeping the crew together."

He pursed his lips, his eyebrows furrowed. "Just kept hoping by some miracle you'd be alive, and here you are."

The heaviness weighed between us. Then I took a breath. No time to be sentimental.

"What news?" I asked again.

"Sereth received word of our ship's attack." Destin

handed me a paper. "She thought you were dead. We all did. She's coming to help out."

I read it quickly.

My Dearest Captain Alaric Galeborne,

I am relieved to hear of your safety.

Dearest? Relieved? Since when did she care about my safety?

Please remember our promise. The twins must be delivered to the King of Corallure, along with the sealed letter.

Best,

Her Majesty High Queen Sereth of Moanalei Kingdom

Crumpled it in my hand. Typical. Cold. Dismissive. Relief that didn't reach the heart. Why was she coming?

The twins.

And, as if reading my thoughts, Destin said, "We found them, Alaric."

"Well where are they now?" I frowned, but my tone never reached the roughness it was before. What did Malia do to me?

"They said they're under orders from Sereth to find a witch here."

"A witch?" I shook my head. There was only one witch around here, at least that I knew of...

"Unbeknownst to us all, they're witch hunters," said Destin. "They wouldn't tell us much, but from what they did say, Sereth has trained them. They hunt and kill witches. When Sereth's messenger came with a letter for us, he asked for the twins. We told them we couldn't find them, so he went off looking for them. Sounds like he had a message for them too."

Thatcher suddenly appeared and folded his arms. "We found them though, and we got bits of their message from him."

"How long ago?"

"Yesterday."

"What did he tell them?" I demanded.

Destin spoke first. "They refused to come with us because they are under orders from Sereth–"

"They're looking for a witch," Thatcher cut in, then pulled up his sleeve, revealing a large gash, which had mostly healed. "The girl gave me this when I tried to detain her. I don't doubt their abilities. Lilo said they weren't obligated to stay with us."

The cut seemed intentional, like Lilo could have gone deeper if she wanted, but she only sliced his skin. A warning.

"So she wants me to take the twins to the king and queen yet Sereth gave them their own separate orders?" I shook my head. Things were not adding up. Wouldn't she have commanded them to return to me immediately?

Destin made a face. "And speaking of witches, sounds like they're going after the witch here."

"Which one?" Thatcher joked. "This place is full of crazy heads. There's that girl you're in love with, Alaric. But there's more. There's a man–might as well call him a witchy madman–who claims oil can be *drilled* from the shores throughout the Tempest Seas."

For a moment, I paused the conversation. Oil could be... drilled? Not harvested by whales?

"Really?"

"You don't actually believe him!" Thatcher laughed, then frowned. "Do you?"

What if?

"Where is this man?" I asked.

My navigator raised an eyebrow. "Met him at the pub the other day. You don't really believe him, do you?"

I swallowed hard.

"If there's a way to obtain oil without killing whales..." I started to say, when Thatcher folded his arms.

"She's one of *them,* isn't she? A whale lover?"

"What?" I looked up.

"That witch?"

I shook my head, returning to our conversation. I'd think about the oil-drilling madman later.

Right now, *that* witch might be in danger.

Malia.

My shoulders tightened. "What are they saying about Malia?"

Destin ran his hands through his dark hair, looking around to make sure nobody was listening. Then he leaned in again. "They said not to make eye contact or she'll put a curse on you. They say she worships darkness and lives in the woods alone. Some said she's beautiful, but if you get too close she'll kill you."

"Someone else said she fled from Moanalei," added Thatcher. "And she's hiding from Sereth."

"Sereth?" I blinked. What was Malia hiding?

But this is nonsense. I lived with her for days now and she did nothing but help me, serve me, and help me heal.

Yet, glancing at Thatcher's cut, I knew Malia was not safe. She had to be warned.

My closest friends frowned. "You look like you've seen a ghost," said my cousin.

Not a ghost. Pieces began coming together.

Malia.

Two children she once housed.

The burn marks...

It *had* to be them.

And they were coming for her.

I stood, the pain in my side severe from the sudden movement, but I had to go. The kids could be anywhere.

"So they're going after Malia?" More a statement than a question.

Destin swallowed. "They didn't say her name specifically, but they said she lives in a cottage in the woods not too far from here. Calls herself an herb witch. So..." He nodded. "I don't know any other witches around here."

Fear cut through the exhaustion like a blade. "I have to find her."

She needed to be warned. No, protected until I could talk to Sereth or the twins myself.

"You have to find those twins and detain them until Sereth gets here," I said. "I don't care what she ordered them to do. Take care of the crew, and I'll meet you back at the inn once I know Malia is safe."

Destin frowned. "Are you going back?"

"He loves her, can't you tell?" Thatcher teased. "Why don't you just marry her, Alaric?"

"I don't love anyone," I snarled, the words tasting like a lie on my tongue. "She's just a loose end that needs tying."

I shoved past them, ignoring Thatcher's smirk and Destin's furrowed brows, and headed for the forest. My pulse pounded like the surf in a storm. Every moment wasted was another chance for the twins to reach her first.

As I passed the booths, I kept an eye out for a dagger to purchase. Before I left, Destin threw me a bag of coins.

Smart man. Always thinking a step ahead.

This was good.

I'd make sure Malia was safe, and I could repay her.

But first... a weapon.

Unfortunately, this was one of those quaint coastal towns. Peaceful. Artistic.

Wooden and shell jewelry sat out on display. Glass art and painted canvases stretched out amongst the booths. Koa bowls waited to be bought.

There are no weapons here... And even if there were, it'd be a hefty price. I should've asked Destin or Thatcher if they had a dagger I could borrow, or look in our stores if we had any extras.

The banyan trees stood like wooden statues. They reached towards the sky, yet their roots and branches dangled off like skeletal fingers, taking root in the ground again.

I kept scanning the crowds, wondering if I might see the twins or the dark haired witch.

As soon as I told her, and made sure she was safe, I'd go back to the inn, stay with my men, and return to Moanalei. This whole thing would be a deal of the past.

The assassin and ambush situation would hopefully resolve itself too.

I walked through the banyan trees, finding a group of children at play. They held hands and danced in a circle, with one child in the middle. They chanted:

Ring around the banyan tree,

The witch is coming—count to three!

One, two, three!

When they finished counting, the child in the middle tried to reach out and grab the hand of someone in the circle.

I'd never heard the chant before or seen this game.

But I knew who they spoke of, and it angered me. Had anyone *tried* to get to know Malia?

The children began another chant.

Hide your brothers, hide your sisters,

Or Malia will make them dinner!

"Some say she ate children," a voice quietly said behind me. It was a woman, selling flowers at her booth, who gossiped with her customer.

"I heard she found herself a whaler," another said.

"Maybe she put a spell on him," said another.

"How can she place a spell when she can't even see him?" The women snickered and I glared at them.

Anger welled up in me.

I have to find her.

THE WALK back nearly killed me. Each step pulled at the wound in my side, but I kept going.

Through groves and tangled paths and gullies washed from rain. Malia's cottage rose like a mirage through the trees.

I barely managed a knock before the door swung open and her eyes widened in alarm. "Alaric?"

Her eyes were red, like she'd been crying.

"Malia..." I leaned against the door frame, exhaustion tearing me down.

"They're coming," I rasped. "The twins. I had to—" My vision swam, and the world tipped.

I felt her arms catch me. Felt her warm, vanilla scent envelop me.

And then everything went dark.

WHEN I CAME TO, I was on the settee, a blanket over my shoulders and the scent of herbs thick in the air.

The smell of soup filled the cottage and when I stepped

into the doorway of the kitchen, I found Malia back to her usual self, humming and cutting a mango. Her head was turned slightly, and she held the mango at an odd angle while she scooped out the insides.

Then she noticed me there and jumped. Again, she never met my eyes, but, instead, turned her head slightly, as if she were gazing at me from the side of her face, to look me up and down.

"You clean up nicely," she said.

"Thanks." I rubbed my chin, feeling a little self-conscious and hoping I didn't miss any spots while shaving.

"Would you happen to have a dagger I can borrow?" I asked.

She gave me a side look. "Why?"

"To protect you." I quickly added, "And me. In case someone attacks."

She paused, placed her finger on her lip, as if thinking, then nodded and brushed past me, her arm touching my chest as we both somehow fit in the kitchen doorway.

"Is that why you came back?" she asked, taking my wrist and leading me to her room. She had a humble bed with an old, ratted quilt. A little nightstand sat next to it, made of old wood scraps. A lantern sat on top of a stack of books. But something else caught my attention: a small wooden ship.

The sides of it were worn and smooth, as if a child had played with it for years. Was it Malia's...

Or the children's toy?

The twins...

She looked under the bed, then let out a sigh. "It's so hard to see."

"Let me help," I said, kneeling.

"It's in the chest with a golden lock."

The light was dim, but not terribly so. I found it easily.

Malia slipped a key from her apron and opened the chest, handing me a dagger.

It did not come from someone living on the streets. It contrasted the poverty-like cottage around us. Instead of bland colors and outdated designs, the golden dagger hilt was bejeweled. The sheath was made of the finest leather and embedded with dazzling jewels. I pulled it out, noting just how shiny the blade was.

It had never been used.

"Where did you get this?"

"My father gifted it to me when I was a little girl. Said I should always keep it in case someone tries to hurt me." She shrugged as she continued preparing food. "Discovered quickly that I wouldn't need it. There are worse ways to be hurt than with a physical weapon."

Ouch. I watched her for a moment, the internal struggle waging.

I need to warn her.

I followed her. "The twins are coming after you, Malia. You need to–"

"I know, Alaric." She didn't cut me off often. "It's none of your worry. So why don't you just enjoy a meal before heading back to your crew, alright?" Malia touched my arm, looking at me in her strange way. "Thank you for warning me... I had a feeling they'd find me."

"Why, though? What did you really do to them?"

"We can talk later." She returned to preparing food.

I hesitated. She was set on *not* talking about this now.

So...

"Can I help in here?" I asked, almost... *embarrassed.* I was a whaler.

Didn't do domestic things like this.

Yet, I felt I needed to.

I wanted to.

I owed her so much.

"Sure." She motioned for me to cut a pineapple. We worked in a content silence, something that was... different.

Much to my surprise, I *liked* it.

When Malia passed me to check on the soup boiling over the fire, she hesitated next to me, then leaned closer.

"What are you doing?"

"You smell like the sea." Her voice was thoughtful.

I raised an eyebrow. "So?"

"I like it."

I stared at her, watched the way she tucked her hair behind her ear. She wasn't even looking at me, just lost in her thoughts. She continued humming and returned to whatever she was doing, and I realized *this* is what was killing me. She was fascinated by me, and it was showing. Could this mean...

I shook my head and quickly turned my attention to the pineapple. I'd never cut one of these before, but, because she didn't say anything, I assumed I was doing it right.

I was used to fileting fish or skinning a sea animal, not cutting fruit.

"Here, try this. I think it's missing something." With spoon in hand, Malia blew on it before reaching up and putting it into my mouth. It was such a foreign move, I froze. I wasn't used to being fed, wasn't used to being a kitchen, wasn't used to having a pretty girl care about my opinion on such a domestic topic...

"Too hot?" Her eyes went wide.

"No, no..." And that's when I realized the soup was shockingly good. Something about this simple act of someone making something for me was messing with my brain and heart.

"So? How is it?" she asked, her voice eager.

I suddenly wanted to walk away, to get out of here. What was happening to me? Something inside of me was... healing. I was being fed, not just physically.

"It's..." I was so distraught and delighted by these new feelings, it became overwhelming. "It's very good, Malia."

Before she could respond, there was a knock on the door, as if someone knocked in haste. Instinctively, I grabbed the hilt of the dagger and stood in front of her. "I'll get it."

She nodded and followed me.

I opened the door. A woman stood there, eyes wide. For a beat, she just stared.

Then,"Is the witch here?" she asked, frantic.

"I'm here," Malia said, brushing past me. "Samantha, right?" How did Malia know the woman's name?

Then it hit me.

She cared about others, knew about the people in the village. But they only shafted her.

It made my insides seethe with anger, and all I wanted to do was prove to everyone that Malia was not a bad person. She was *not* the villain.

The woman clutched a basket. "Yes. I don't have coins, but I brought these." She lifted the lid, revealing baked goods, fruits, and vegetables. Her hands shook. "I'll pay what I can later. Please—"

"What's wrong?" Malia's voice softened. Like she'd done this before. Probably had.

"My son. He cut himself on the reef a few days ago. Now he's burning up. The doctor said there's nothing more we can do." Her voice cracked. "Please. I don't know where else to go."

"Wait here."

Malia slipped past me into the kitchen. I followed.

She moved fast, already gathering bottles, tins, small cloth-wrapped bundles of herbs. "I'll be back soon," she said over her shoulder. "The soup's nearly ready. Just stir it now and then. Let the fire die low. Eat something. Rest."

There was something in her tone. A motherly gentleness that I hadn't felt in years.

Felt like family. And maybe something more.

It twisted something in my chest.

She loaded her basket quickly, then paused and looked up at me.

There it was again—that strange way she saw me. Like she wasn't quite looking at me... and yet, somehow, she was.

"He likely has an infection," she said. "If I get this to him fast enough, there's still a chance."

"Wait," I said, grabbing her arm. "Those twins are out there–"

"Alaric." She slipped her arm away and squeezed my hand. "I'll be fine. You need to rest. We can talk later."

And then she was out the door, her words trailing behind her like wind. She talked to Samantha as she walked, explaining things to the woman who hurried to keep up.

I stood there, leaning against the frame, arms crossed. Watching her. The way she moved. Purposeful, calm, certain.

They called her witch.

But all I saw was someone who helped without hesitation.

Her hair caught in the breeze as she walked down the dirt path. And then she turned.

She waved.

No one had ever waved to me before.

I stared, caught off guard. Then I lifted a hand and waved back.

And just like that, I knew.

I was starting to care.

And I shouldn't.

I was a whaler. A huntsman. I lived at sea.

And, unfortunately, that life didn't leave space for this.

CHAPTER TEN

MALIA

I returned when the moon shone through the windows and the crickets chirped.

I found Alaric on the settee, asleep.

Good. He needed the rest, especially after the long, strenuous walk today.

His long strenuous walk to find me...

And he didn't have to tell me everything. I knew the twins were coming for me.

It was overwhelming. Should I stay? Should I flee?

I rubbed my temple, too exhausted to think clearly. My thoughts were like mud mixing into water.

Much to my surprise, the kitchen was all cleaned up, the soup put away in one of my wooden containers. I glanced at the whaler, his expression peaceful as he slept.

After he groomed and cleaned himself up, I couldn't deny that he was even more attractive.

Malia, that's so wrong, I thought. But was it?

A yawn escaped and I sleepily washed up for the night. I should've warmed some food up and ate, hungry as I was, but I was also too tired. The fireplace was going, and the night had turned rather chilly. I sat in the rocking chair and fell asleep.

"MALIA." A warm blanket wrapped around my shoulders, and when I opened my eyes, Alaric knelt next to my chair, a bowl of steaming soup in his hands.

I blinked wearily. "You should be resting."

The corner of his lip twitched, like he almost found this amusing. "I was resting. You should eat something."

I was suddenly *very* awake. When was the last time someone cared for me? I grabbed the blanket self consciously. He'd done that too!

"Thank you..." I was so shocked, it took me a minute to start eating. Alaric got comfortable on the settee again, and I tried not to look at him too many times, my suspicion of him growing. Why was he being so nice? Surely there was some hidden meaning beneath it.

"Was the boy alright?" he asked, and I nodded.

"His wound was infected but I really think the salve will help. I made him some turmeric tea to help with the swelling and..." I paused, surprised that Alaric's gaze was still on me, as if he found it all interesting... as if he found *me* interesting. "You keep looking at me like that," I said, not finishing my story.

He raised an eyebrow. "Like what?"

"Like you're..." I shrugged. "Like you're thinking about something..."

His jaw clenched. "Like what?"

"I don't know." I tilted my head and smiled, not knowing why I found this amusing. "Like you're thinking about me?"

He exhaled slowly and ran a hand over his face. "Maybe. We need to talk."

I nodded. "We will."

And then he was studying me, his gaze moving to my lips, my hands, and I became even more self conscious. Was he studying my eyes? When would he ask about it? Or would he? The thought made my stomach twist. What would he say if I told him the truth about my eyesight?

A muscle ticked in his jaw and my heart skipped a beat. "You should rest," he said, his voice hoarse.

"You too." I don't know what overcame me, but we'd never spoken *playfully* like this before. It was the first time I felt... in control. Like he really didn't know what to do around me, like there might be something deep inside of him that had feelings for me.

Perhaps it was wishful thinking.

But still... for whatever reason, it thrilled me.

THE NEXT DAY, I suggested we take a walk along the beach to help Alaric get his strength back. Maybe I also hoped he would tell me whatever it was he wanted to say the previous night.

He slept in awfully late, a testament to the after-effects of yesterday's long walk. But now, walking barefoot along the white sand beach, I couldn't help but notice just how alive and healthy he looked. His warm tan, his dark hair, his toned arms–it was all such a stark difference to the first time I saw him.

The waves lapped playfully along the shore, the sun shone in the sky, and the mist and splashes of whales portrayed a beautiful sight in the distance.

Alaric put his hands in his pockets while I carried a

small basket to collect shells and sea glass I found along the way.

He was quiet, his jaw set, like he was thinking again. After I picked up a few *puka* shells and showed him, I looked up to see him studying me, not the shells. "Why were those children chanting about you yesterday, Malia? Is that why you were crying when I found you?"

Oh. Is that what he wanted to talk about?

My heart sank. "Maybe... People like to find someone to tease and fear. It just happens to be me."

"Why would they even come up with a chant about you eating children?" He frowned. "That's so... revolting."

My heart sank further, as if it wasn't already buried in the deepest part of the island. I shrugged and kept walking. Before Alaric could ask more questions about my being a witch, I pointed to the distance.

"Look."

Humpback whales breached in the sea, causing white splashes that misted away in the wind. Their tails were beautiful as they dove up and down, water shooting from their blowholes.

"I used to think the whales sang just for me," I said. Alaric stood next to me, close enough now that his arm touched mine. His sleeves were rolled up, revealing his muscular forearms. He folded his arms and watched the whales.

"When I was little, I'd sneak to the shore in the mornings and sit for hours, listening," I continued, not sure why I was sharing this with him. What did he care? Yet I said it anyway. "They were... the only ones who weren't out to hurt me. I loved listening to them and imagined that they cared enough to listen to me too."

Alaric looked at me. "You're always someone worth listening to."

My breath hitched and I quickly looked away, allowing my curtain of hair to hide my face from his view. The waves continued to beat against the shore, rushing past our ankles. My heart pounded, and it took me a moment to respond.

"There are nights I wonder why I'm still here. Why I was spared. I feel like a ghost of someone I was meant to be. I feel like... just... leftovers."

Another whale breached, twisting so one moment we saw its white underbelly and the next its deep blue back. I blinked fast, knowing I should stop talking. I was making a fool of myself and proving the very fact that nobody cared to listen to me. But I wanted to finish my thought anyway, because what if? What if Alaric didn't mind listening to me?

"But when I hear them. The whales... I wonder—maybe Akua didn't forget me. Maybe He kept me here for a reason. I just... haven't seen it yet."

Alaric stepped closer, carefully, as if any wrong move might shatter me. Now we were facing each other and my heart was pounding so loudly, I was sure he could hear it.

"You're not leftovers, Malia," he said. "You're the reason I'm still standing." And then he did something I was not expecting. He gently took my hand, his fingers interlacing mine, and squeezed it. Not possessively, not boldly. Reverently.

And just as soon as he held it, he let go and looked away, color in his cheeks. I looked away too, letting the sea fill the silence. A mixture of awareness and awkwardness seemed to charge between Alaric and I. We were standing too close. He just took my hand. And all I could think was, *What does it mean?* I did not understand what was happening, but, more confusing than that, I was both terrified and delighted at the same time.

LATER THAT EVENING, I kneaded some dough, trying to sort through my thoughts. There was a festival in town the following day, and Noni recommended I give her some baked goods to sell. I was making a lot of money from the markets, which would help with much needed repairs for my cottage.

So I was motivated, plus I needed something to distract me.

Alaric and I both had been nearly silent the entire rest of the walk, the entire rest of the evening. He should have rested, exhaustion wearing on him from the walk, but, instead, he went out and chopped wood. He said exercising–not resting–would help him recover faster.

Meanwhile, I made bread. I heard him go to the washroom to get cleaned up, but I tried to focus on the task at hand.

Except my mind wasn't on the bread. It was on him. The way he took my hand, the way it felt. Nobody had *ever* held my hand. I couldn't even recall holding my mother's hand. Yet he'd taken my hand. *My* hand!

Despite my excitement about his tender gesture, I knew he wouldn't leave until we talked about the twins, which terrified me. It was the unspoken, unfinished business we had between us, like a vine choking a tree.

"Do you always work like that?"

I gasped and now noticed that Alaric was watching me from the doorway of the kitchen, arms folded, one brow arched.

"Like what?"

"Like the bread's about to run off the table."

I fought a smile. That was a funny way to describe it. "I suppose I have my own way."

Then Alaric stepped forward, his voice quiet but solid. "You never look straight at things. Not the bread. Not me. I thought maybe it was shyness."

Shyness? I blushed at that.

His voice dropped. "But I think it's something else."

I didn't move, my fingers sticky with dough. I turned back to my work, dusting my hands with flour. "It's not too bad." I said it too quickly.

Alaric waited. He didn't press, and that made my heart hammer. He moved to my side, taking my flour dusted hand and lifting it gently, then he adjusted my chin with his other hand so I was looking more directly at him, if just off-center. How did he know I could see him better this way? "Can you see me better this way, Malia?"

I nodded slowly, my throat tightening. I had to stop this. Now! The whaler was wedging his way into my heart, whether he meant it or not.

"You have nice hands," I said. I meant it. They were scarred, tanned, and calloused.

Alaric blinked, the magical moment disappearing like dust on a windy day. "Pardon?"

I shrugged, trying to play off the intense moment. "They're strong."

A long pause, as if Alaric were reading me, reading that I was fighting this attraction to him. And he knew better than to feed it, instead of fight it.

He exhaled sharply. "You're trouble, witch."

"I know."

But none of us moved for a moment. Then Alaric let out another quiet breath, changing the subject.

"Was there anything else you needed help with?"

I forced a smile and nodded, searching for something... anything... for him to do.

His jaw set. He flexed his fingers as if trying to shake something out of them. I knew this was dangerous... *he* was feeling it too.

But we weren't meant to be, a whaler and a witch, and it killed me inside.

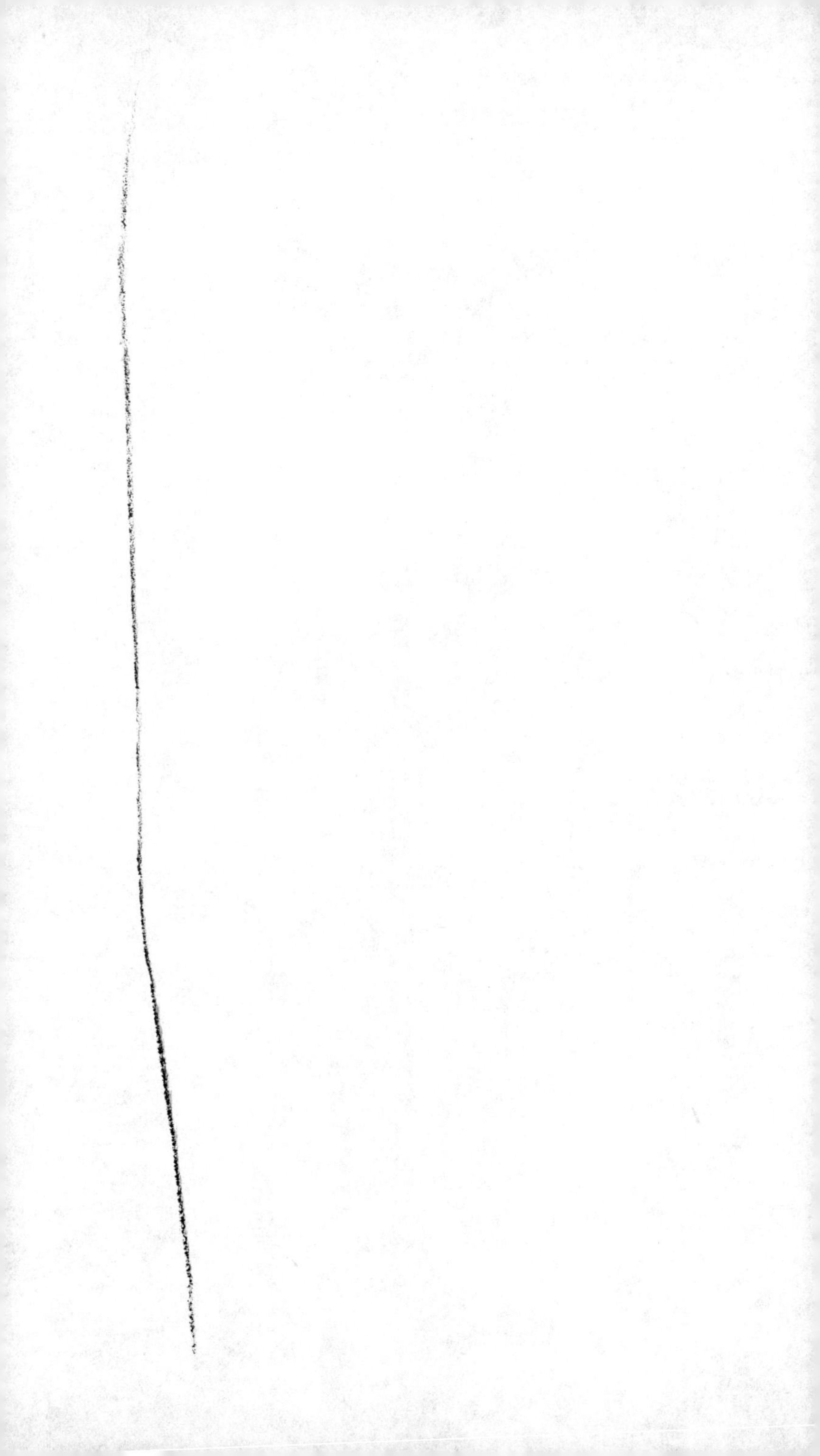

CHAPTER ELEVEN
ALARIC

We have to talk.

I was well enough to leave, but I had to tell Malia about the witch hunters. When I surveyed the cottage, I found it was much more rundown than I first imagined. She'd never be safe here.

Anybody could barge in at any time.

I could leave more than enough money to help her patch up the place. But that was not the answer… her living conditions were not good, and, at any moment, a storm could rip her cottage to pieces. It was a miracle it still stood.

As I sat on the settee, thinking this, Malia tended to the fire, humming like she always did. I caught myself watching her, the way her hair fell down either side of her face, sometimes blocking it from view, the way she was so ordinary and domestic yet…

It hit me like a splash of cold water in the morning. A wake up call.

I'm done for.

I didn't mean to stare, but I did. I'd seen beautiful women before but Malia? She was different. The way she moved so effortlessly, the way her lips curved just slightly when she was lost in thought, the way she hummed and enjoyed being in the present moment.

Something in my chest tightened.

I realized the truth.

Oh blast it. I had kept myself from cursing, but a slew of curses rattled off in my head.

It's her... it's always been her. I looked away, frustrated at such a revelation. I had gotten involved with other women in the past, something I was *not* proud of. But it had been surfacey, based on lust and physical attraction. With Malia, it was so much more. So much deeper.

But I can't stay. I had my whaling empire to get back to. I had a life any man would dream of.

I have to warn her and then leave.

Besides, I had faced the truth long ago. Domestic life wasn't for me. It never had been. I was too rough. My hands were too dirty to live a life like this... and especially with her. Furthermore, I wouldn't be the failure that my father was.

I made up my mind.

I'm leaving. After the festival tonight and delivering her goods with her, I'd be on my way.

Yes.

LIGHTS HUNG from the banyan trees. The Halekai square was full of people. Music filled the air and I followed Malia as she wove through the crowd, her hand on my wrist. She had struggled the entire way, veering off the path multiple times, tripping on roots. She finally took my arm and I led the way to town. She didn't have to say it, but I knew it was her eyes. I wished she would tell me what happened, or if it had always been that way, but she didn't.

It killed me that after tonight, she'd have to stumble home.

Because I'm leaving her. Or I could walk her home... a fierce protectiveness made me want to do that, but my head knew better. If I didn't leave tonight, I might not leave at all.

"There's Noni," Malia said after a long while

She'd been searching the crowd, looking at things in her strange way.

I wish I'd helped Malia look for her friend. All I could do was scan the crowd, wondering if the twins might jump out at any moment.

The witch let go of my hand. "I'll be back. Don't get too lost, please." She smiled warmly and left me there.

I folded my arms and looked around, aware of the Corallure guards standing across the crowd of dancers. They seemed relaxed, as though they were here for a good time too.

A laugh pulled me from my thoughts.

Malia stood beneath the banyan tree, talking to a young man: chestnut hair, dressed like royalty.

Prince Elias.

I stepped closer to the trunk, hoping he wouldn't see me. What was she doing talking to him?

I'd met Elias once, back when he married Sereth, not long after I chose to rescue her from her stepmother. The rumor was she bit into a poisoned apple, and he broke the spell with a kiss. Their marriage didn't last. He couldn't stomach her practices.

Some say Sereth made her stepmother dance in red-hot

shoes until she dropped dead. Others say she killed the queen outright. No one knows for sure.

Elias left the lush mountains and army-ridden lands of Moanalei and returned to the tourist-trap and pristine beaches of Corallure. They hadn't seen each other since: not really husband and wife, not really divorced.

He said something that made Malia smile.

Something twisted in my chest. A sharp, sour feeling I hated. I wanted to march over there and knock that stupid smirk off his face, but I didn't move.

Malia can talk to whoever she wants.

Then why did it bother me so much that she was talking to him?

She gestured to the loaves she was selling, laughing at something he said. Then they kissed each other's cheeks and parted ways.

It was nothing. Just a custom.

Still, it made my blood boil. Made my thoughts simmer in disgust that she wasn't someone I could claim. Never was.

And yet, Elias could make her smile so easily. Did he even really know her? Did he taste her home cooked meals or listen to her gentle humming? Did he know how gracefully she moved and how gently she touched? He didn't know a thing about her.

Or so I secretly hoped.

I fought the urge to march up to him and shove him to the ground just as a warning to *stay away.*

But I couldn't.

Malia and I had never kissed like that. Not even as a greeting.

And suddenly, I wanted it. Maybe more. Badly.

I'd already made my decision.

So why wouldn't the feelings die?

"So that's what you've been up to." Destin's voice sounded close to me. I turned and glared at him, but his attention was riveted on Malia. "Are you sure she hasn't cast a spell on you?"

"Are you sure you don't want this fist in your face?" I warned, and Destin rubbed his chin.

"She's beautiful, Alaric, but..."

"But what?"

"You can't have her and the sea."

The dark truth. Destin said it out loud, and it killed me. Made me feel like I was drowning. No air. And there was no way to swim out of this mess.

"Did you find the twins?" I asked, changing the subject.

"I've asked around. A couple of villagers have seen them."

I touched the dagger at my side. *They must be here then...* My attention went straight to Malia, watching her every move.

I can't let anything happen to her.

"Keep an eye out," I said to Destin and he nodded, excusing himself as she began to approach.

When the witch reached me, the smile on her face disappeared slowly. It made my shoulders tighten. Why didn't she smile around me? Did I scare her, just as I scared everyone else?

"Were you talking to someone?" she asked.

I hesitated, and her cheeks colored. "You're most welcome to dance with any of the women here if you'd like, Alaric. I think I'm going to walk home now though."

I didn't want to dance with any of the women here.

Just her.

“Let’s dance,” I said, not thinking, and she blushed again.

“I don’t dance. I mean... I haven’t danced in years.”

“Good.” I took her hand and led her into the circle. My mother taught me to dance when I was younger, and, much to my surprise, Malia seemed to know the moves as well. It was an island waltz, which was fast enough for things not to get awkward, but slow enough that I could hold her close to me and we could talk.

She danced like a princess, as if she’d been trained to do this.

“Was that the prince you spoke to?” I asked.

She nodded. “Yes. He was my first customer to buy baked goods and he’s enjoyed them ever since.”

My jaw tightened. *Stupid prince.* Well I’d been enjoying more than just her baked goods. She made meals and snacks and if only he knew what an incredible cook she was...

Stop, Alaric. But I couldn’t.

“Is something bothering you?” Malia asked. “You seem... tense, like someone’s going to rob your ship.”

Oh yes. I was very tense. “Maybe someone did rob my ship.”

Then her eyebrows raised, as if she realized something. “What would you do if I kissed you?” The question came out of nowhere, and it sent my head reeling.

“What? You wouldn’t?”

“Wouldn’t I?” She leaned in, just a fraction. Enough to make my hands curl into fists.

“Don’t.”

She leaned back, then said. “I want to try something.” And just like that, she pressed a soft kiss to my jaw. I inhaled sharply, my whole world turning upside down. She searched my face, and then the softest smile touched her lips.

I was done for.

I grabbed her hand and led her out of the circle, walking through the quiet streets until we reached an empty alley.

I'd had all these plans to leave. I'd rehearsed what I'd say, a hundred times over. But the words slipped away the moment I silently admitted my feelings for her.

I braced one hand on the stone archway behind her, caging her in—not to trap her, but to keep myself from falling apart.

"Tell me to stop," I whispered.

Her eyes looked past me, wide and unreadable. She didn't move. Didn't speak. Her silence undid me.

"Tell me to leave, Malia." My voice cracked. My nose brushed hers. A breath of contact, nothing more. But she leaned toward me.

"Tell me..." I said.

I knew this was impossible—me, the whaler. Her, the witch. A life divided by sea and spell.

But she said nothing. And that silence was everything.

So I kissed her.

It wasn't careful. It wasn't practiced. It was like giving in to a storm: wild, reckless, the kind a man survives only once.

Her hands found my shoulders, and I nearly lost my grip.

I told myself it would be one kiss. A mistake I could take back. But then her mouth met mine again, and suddenly it was more... too much. My hands found her waist, then her back, trying to memorize the shape of something I was never meant to hold.

I pulled her closer. Closer than I should.

I was losing control.

This wasn't just a kiss. It was a tide. And I was being pulled under.

I broke away, breath ragged, forehead pressed to hers. My whole body shook with restraint.

"I'm sorry," I whispered. "Malia, I'm sorry."

She held me close, her eyes shut. "You're leaving." It was more of a statement than a question, and I felt the hurt and heartache beneath her words.

She would never ask me to stay.

She knew me... my life... the blood on my hands.

Her fingers clutched the fabric of my shirt, as she buried her face in my chest, hot tears kissing my skin.

"Thank you for everything, Malia, but... I can't stay," I said again, the unspoken truth wedging between us, a barnacle clinging fast to the hull of a sinking ship. My heart was pounding like war drums before a storm, and my blood pulsed through my veins like tidewater through a broken dam.

I wanted to stay.

Wanted this life with her.

But I could never be the man she wants and needs.

I pulled away, leaving her there alone.

Go back, Alaric! My heart raged at me. But it was silly to think we could work out. I belonged on my ship at sea, commanding fleets and men to obey my every word. We were too different: her softness, my rigidness.

Her kindness, my cruelty.

Her innocence, my shame.

Her beauty, my beastliness.

I stormed down the street, knowing this was how it had to end... even though every inch of me wanted to turn around and be with her again.

When I turned the corner, I stopped and took a deep breath, gazing out at the dark sea. So that was our goodbye. The kiss.

I rubbed my forehead and looked up at the stars. I wasn't a very religious man, but I began to wonder, like Malia, why Akua allowed me to survive this long. There were many close encounters in my life, and many shreds of luck or coincidences that allowed me to survive.

Just like the whale with the white tail...

Taking a deep breath I rubbed my face again. *What am I to do?*

Go back to my whaling life... Go back where I belonged. Yes.

Just as I made up my mind and began pacing down the street, a sound pierced the night air.

A scream.

Not just any scream... *her* scream. I whirled on my heels and sprinted back to where I came.

"Malia!"

CHAPTER TWELVE
MALIA

I had nothing to defend myself with, except to scream. "Help! *Alaric!*" He was probably long gone, a feeling that hurt more than the wound inflicted on me. He would forever be in my heart.

I'd never forget that kiss.

But now...

Crimson coated my right shoulder and collarbone, where the stinging sensation told me the wound was more than just a cut.

Poison.

Two tall teenagers stood before me, daggers in hand.

"How did you get away?" the girl asked, her face pale, her fingers tight around the hilt of her dagger. She was so much older than the last time we met, a testament of how much time had passed.

How long I've been hiding.

They were children when they came to my home, and now they were teenagers. I clung to my knees, at the mercy of these children... *again.* Last time they'd trapped me in the furnace and this time they trapped me in the alleyway. I shook like a leaf, panic washing over me.

"I got out," I managed to say, my hair falling all around me.

"Let's just finish her," said Niko. "In case she gets away again."

Lilo hesitated though.

"Remember what she did," he reminded her, but she shook her head.

"Niko, she was so kind to us..."

"She poisoned Sereth," Niko said and I quickly shot back.

"She tricked me into making the apple. You have to believe me–I would never hurt you."

Lilo still hesitated, and I could see the conflict in her eyes. Niko was set though, manipulated by Snow White. They served Sereth, and loved Sereth. She wooed them, just as she wooed everyone.

Just as she wooed Alaric too. I wasn't ignorant to the fact that his reputation was built because he saved Sereth's life...

Everything seemed to revolve around her, the "fairest of them all." And now I was going to die because everyone believed her lies. Was this how I really wanted it to end? What if the world knew the truth about her?

But I can't... Nobody had ever believed me.

They always believed her... ever since we were younger...

I swallowed hard. Now was not the time to think of this. Now I had reached the end. I squeezed my eyes shut, hoping it wouldn't hurt to die.

Instead, I tried to hold onto the romantic exchange just moments before. The first time in my life I actually felt loved and valued. Yes, Alaric had left and walked away, but he left me with a gift I would treasure before death.

Before I closed my eyes, I noticed that Lilo's dark eyes were tired, like *she* was tired of this. Niko, meanwhile, looked hungry for revenge. Revenge for what though? I'd done nothing but care for them.

Perhaps, after all this time, his heart had been hardened, rather than softened.

I felt sorry for him.

For both of them.

"I'm sorry it has to end this way," I said, scooting back against the wall and covering my face as they both stepped forward, their shadows falling on me. "I loved you both," I said, and that undid Lilo.

She took a step back, turned to Niko to finish the job.

"I'm sorry too," she said, avoiding eye contact.

Niko stepped forward, dagger glinting in the moonlight. My breath hitched and I kept my eyes closed.

Then... footsteps came dashing up the street. Before any of us could react, the whaler shoved Niko to the ground.

Lilo screamed. "You!"

"Don't touch her!" Alaric's large frame and build were enough to scare off any predator. Niko tried to attack with his dagger, but the whaler was quicker. He knocked the dagger out of Niko's hand and grabbed his shirt.

"I can snap your twiggy neck right now," Alaric threatened.

"No! Let him go!" Lilo grabbed Alaric's arm, but it did nothing. His eyes flashed towards me, and, upon seeing me cornered and wounded like a fish caught in a net, he snatched Lilo's wrist. "Who are you both really? What did you do?"

Fear coated Lilo's voice as she quickly said, "She's going

to die, Captain Alaric. She's been poisoned and if you don't help her within the hour, it'll kill her..." Almost as if she were trying to help.

That's when he let them go, rushing to me. "Malia." He scooped me into his arms, as if I didn't weigh a thing. "*Malia...*"

"Hurry!" Lilo grabbed Niko's coat and scrambled away into the darkness of the streets before the whaler ran after them.

"No, don't carry me... your wound," I said, trying to stand, but I suddenly felt very sick. Feverish. Shaky.

"I'm carrying you." Alaric's voice was breathy. "They hurt you..." He cursed and looked after the twins as he said, "I should've never left you."

I wrapped my arms around his neck and buried my face in his warm chest, the whalebone necklace right in front of me, as if reminding me of the reality of our situation.

"You came back," I whispered, tears streaming down my cheeks.

He pressed his forehead against mine, as if searching for words but not knowing what to say. He was conflicted, and it put a wedge even deeper into my heart.

"There's medicine," I said quietly. "At my cottage."

His lips suddenly caught mine and his few light kisses set my world on fire. "Hang in there, witch." A small smile formed on my face, and I allowed myself to be carried by him, worried as I was about his wound and his strength. But it didn't take long for us to return to the cottage, and I was amazed that he remembered the path so well.

When we got inside, he placed me on the settee and I gave him directions on where to find the salve. I could smell the poison, knowing exactly what it was, but my mind was growing delirious.

Alaric sat behind me on the settee, gently moving my hair to one side. "Can you take this off? At least so I can clean this up?" he asked, and self consciousness flooded me. I slipped the right sleeve off my shoulder, holding the front of my dress for modesty. I knew I needed to change, my dress soiled from the blood and poison, but having to remove my clothing–if only partially–felt much too intimate.

I closed my eyes and tried to get rid of that thought.

Alaric was only tending to me, as I had once tended to him. An exhale escaped sharply as he ran a damp cloth over my bare shoulder.

"Does it hurt?" he asked, his voice lower than usual.

"Not really." In fact, the entire area felt numb. Once he cleaned the wound and applied the salve, I let out a sigh of relief.

"I'll be alright," I said, my cheeks still hot, and not just from the fever.

It was him. His touch. His kiss. I had fallen in love, and I was angry at myself for it. I shouldn't have... After Alaric bandaged up my wound, he didn't move away. Instead, he cleaned the rest of the blood that had stained my back and neck.

I sat still as a statue.

Alaric...

I wanted him, there was no doubt in my mind about it.

We don't belong together. Then why did it feel like I'd lose so much of me once he walked out the door?

I went into my bedroom and changed into clean clothes, then returned to the settee and clumsily began braiding my hair. It was getting caught on the bandage on my shoulder, and that annoyed me.

"Here, let me do it." Alaric didn't even hesitate to braid,

and it was such a sweet thing, such a *tender* thing to do, I melted inside.

"You're hiding something," he said, and I didn't flinch. Instead, I traced the burns on my arms.

"Everyone hides something."

He waited, just as he always did, and it caused more forbidden feelings in my heart.

"It happened five years ago when they came to my home," I said. "They were starving, lost, unwanted. So I fed and took care of them as my own." My vision grew blurry again.

"They tried to kill you?"

"They did kill me." My fingers tightened as I now looked at the flames in the fireplace. I don't know how Alaric started it so quickly. "At least, the person I was before."

Alaric studied me for a long time. Then he placed his arm behind me and gently scooted me closer to him, so my head rested on his chest. I could stay like this forever.

"You're not a monster, Malia."

"To others I am. I am *that* witch, Alaric. The one they say who eats children..."

"It's the reason Sereth started the witch hunt..." Alaric eyed me. "And that's why you've been hiding here in Corallure?"

"Prince Elias knows the truth about me," I confirmed, and the whaler visibly tensed at the mention of Elias.

"It's not like that," I said, then drew closer to Alaric, shivering even though he and the fire were warm. I clutched his shirt and he rubbed my arm. My eyes fluttered as the poison's effects were so intense, I wondered if I might pass out.

"Stay with me, Malia."

Stay with me, *Alaric...* I begged to say it, but I couldn't ask that of him.

"They say you put the boy in a cage and felt his finger to see if he was fattening up," Alaric said, the distaste in his tone obvious. "And when you reached into the cage, he put out a bone for you to feel. What actually happened?"

For some reason, my heart was racing. Nobody had *ever* asked me what happened. Ever! Would he believe me?

"I put a makeshift gate so they couldn't get out of their room until I was awake. Niko would get very upset about little things. I think it was because of their parents abandoning them. He didn't trust me. He didn't trust anyone, and I didn't blame him. But he kept running away into the woods and, at the time, there were a lot of ruffians in the woods. I didn't want him to get kidnapped. Lilo helped me around the house while I sometimes put Niko behind the gate because he was getting too out of hand." I sighed. "I felt so bad, but I was terrified he'd end up in the hands of the ruffians."

"Sereth took care of those ruffians as best as she could," Alaric said. "But I took care of them for good. Took them all and changed them into whalers."

I closed my eyes, knowing this was true. Alaric had single-handedly cleaned up the kingdom more so than Sereth. In fact, he seemed to have cleaned up both kingdoms in the land.

It was why he was so well known. He took orphans and all the unwanted. He took the homeless and the outcasts and made them into something. People adored him, admired him, even honored him. His whaling empire had truly become even more powerful than Sereth the queen and her rule.

"I couldn't see them–" I hesitated. "I can't see anything,

really. So I'd ask them if they were eating enough. They were both so skinny–they still are." My heart saddened for them. They were obviously still serving Sereth as witch hunters, which is what they became after they fled from me and ran to her. But did she feed them? Care for them? They looked exhausted.

"They handed me twigs just because they wanted more food. I would've given them all the food in the world.... I was so sad for them."

"Why did they try to kill you?"

I hesitated, now knowing he wasn't aware of the apple, the poison, and *her*... I swallowed hard.

"They thought I was a bad witch, so..." I swallowed hard. "They threw me in the furnace. I managed to open the door and get out. I was burned. My house burned to the ground, but... I survived. Their father tracked me down. He was ashamed for abandoning them in the woods. He thanked me for taking care of them, and then I escaped. I hid until Prince Elias left Sereth and that's when I spoke to him. He granted me full citizenship in this kingdom."

Alaric's fingers rubbed my shoulder and I wished we could stay like this forever. I clutched his shirt even more tightly and drew closer to him, smelling his sandalwood and fresh sea scent.

"You're the best kind of witch," he said, almost playfully, and I was glad he believed me. A moment of silence passed before he asked, "Have your eyes always been like that?"

"Ever since I was younger." More tears welled up in my eyes.

"It seems hardest for you to see at night, is that right?" he asked.

I nodded. "Any kind of dark spaces... I can't see

anything." And that was when the memory resurfaced. "My sister locked me in a root cellar once," I said. I had never shared it with anyone, but somehow I just *wanted* someone to understand. To know what it felt like to not be able to see, and to have compassion on the little girl who was so terrified.

Who is still terrified. I shivered.

"Your sister?"

"My stepsister," I corrected. "I was always shy, slow to speak, and had difficulty reading or catching visual cues because of... this." I motioned to my eyes. "I was always small. Invisible, even in my own home."

"Even to your mother?"

"Especially to my mother. I think the reason she remarried is because the man had a beautiful daughter. She was perfect." A lump formed in my throat. "Meanwhile, my eyes began to fail me more severely. I struggled to keep up with my studies. I failed in dance lessons. I often fumbled or dropped things. And one day, when we were playing hide-and-seek, my sister locked me in the root cellar." I shuddered. "I was terrified, disoriented. I couldn't see anything. I hurt myself trying to escape and no one believed me when I said my sister did it on purpose."

Alaric's arm slipped away and he rested his elbows on his knees so he could face me, his gaze intent. Serious. Maybe even... angry?

"That's when I learned..." I shook my head, knowing it sounded silly when said out loud. "Hiding is safer, and when one tries to speak up, it does no good. People will never believe me."

"I believe you." Alaric took my hands in his and kissed my knuckles. I wished he would kiss me again, but I knew he was holding himself back. He already said goodbye once, and he was only here because I was injured.

He sat back again and placed his arm around me. We were both quiet for a long time, but his words played over and over in my mind. *I believe you.* When did anyone ever believe me?

He gently spoke after a while. "Want to hear some tales of the sea?"

I nodded, eager to know more about him.

After sharing my own past, I felt vulnerable. And that's when I rested my face on his chest, distracted by his husky voice, his warmth, his genuineness. His stories took me away from my own pain–the present and the past. He told stories of the sea, his childhood, his regrets. The moment was so cozy, like warm tea steeped with wild lemongrass and honey. I fell asleep listening to him, wishing we could do this every night.

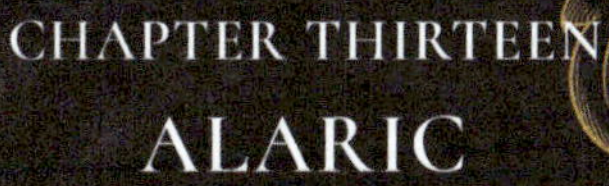

CHAPTER THIRTEEN
ALARIC

Curse this woman. She was slipping into my heart like seawater through the cracks of a ship—and it was driving me mad.

I told myself I wouldn't kiss her again. Once was enough.

I laid her gently in bed and pulled the blanket over her. She looked so peaceful, so soft, it made my chest ache.

This is ridiculous. I was a whaler, forged by storms and salt and solitude. Not someone who sat on settees and whispered sea tales to a woman he shouldn't want.

But I couldn't help it.

When she told me about the rumors, the way people treated her, especially what happened with her sister, I saw her clearly for the first time.

Malia was lonely. Deeply, achingly lonely.

And something inside me tugged like a net caught on coral.

Whaling could be lonely too, sure. But at least we had each other out there.

She had no one. Even Noni kept her distance.

Her only real friend here seemed to be Prince Elias, and that made me jealous with rage.

I sank back into the cushions and shut my eyes, jaw tight. I needed to leave. Sooner rather than later.

As soon as she's well again, I told myself, almost smirking at the turn of the tide.

She once cared for me. Now I could return the favor.

THE NEXT MORNING, I awoke to a cold cottage. Normally Malia woke before me and started the fire. The house would smell like a heavenly breakfast only she could make, and the windows would let in morning sunlight.

But it was quiet. I frowned, then bolted off the settee.

"Malia?" I barged into her room. The bed was empty and unmade, and the washroom door was open. A brief wave of panic came over me. *Did someone kidnap her?* Did the twins come here last night, without me knowing?

I looked in the kitchen and then burst out the front door. That's when I found her, by the well, hunched over, hugging her arms.

"What are you doing?" Anger coated my voice. I didn't mean to sound so mad, but why was she out here?

"I was getting some water to prepare breakfast, but then realized I'm just too tired..." Her braid had become loose and her teeth chattered against each other.

"Come here."

"I'm fine." But her frame trembled like a ship shuddering after a storm.

"You're freezing."

Before she could argue, I scooped her in my arms and

took her inside, holding her body against mine. She stiffened at first, then relaxed.

"I don't know how to be gentle," I admitted, wanting to stroke her back or do something... but I felt awkward. Not used to this. Not used to holding a woman in my arms.

"You're doing fine." Her head rested on my chest.

My grip tightened and I rested my chin lightly on her hair, trying not to enjoy her vanilla scent too much.

"That's the problem, Malia. I don't want to be gentle with you." Or anyone. The only reason I succeeded in my business was because of my cruelty. The whales. My men... Everyone bowed to me. Did what I asked. There was no gentleness in my life.

Until Malia.

Her fingers found my cheek, where she stroked it, as if to show her appreciation. It wasn't anything huge, but it rocked my insides like a storm. Her hand moved down to the whale bone necklace hanging from my neck.

"Once I'm healed, you'll go back, won't you?" she asked softly.

"That was the plan."

She nodded, but something in her face–even when she wasn't looking at me–made my chest tighten.

"And then what?"

I hesitated. No one had ever asked me that before.

Then what? Then I continued building my empire...

What's left to build? I was the wealthiest man in all the kingdoms, with fleets under my command and power and influence that rulers would dream of.

So then what? Maybe *I* hadn't even asked myself that before. After one obtained everything they worked for, where did they go from there?

I let out a quiet breath before saying, "I built a life most men would envy. Wealth. Ships. Power. But... I don't know."

"You're allowed to want more."

Her words pierced me to the core. More? What was *more?* Did she mean a life with her? Settling down? Raising a family? Perhaps part of me never wanted *more* of that because of my parents. My father–also a whaler, albeit a weak one–drowned at sea, leaving my mother behind to raise us. It was hard enough on a whaler's income, but alone? I watched her sink in her sorrows and the stress of providing for me and my siblings.

"I don't even know what more means," I said. Then, quieter, "But I swore I'd never be like my father. Family's not in the cards for me."

Malia tensed, then sighed. "Me either, I think."

"Why not?"

Had she been married? Could she not have children?

As if she heard the question in my silence, she said softly, "I think I'll always be alone. I've made it this far on my own. Why would anyone stay for me?"

Guilt flooded me, thick and heavy, like rotting seawater in the brig.

I shut my eyes. The battle inside me surged like a storm tide.

I wouldn't become my father. I couldn't risk breaking someone the way he broke us. I'd accepted that when I chose this life at sea.

Which meant I had to leave Malia.

But she deserved more than loneliness. She deserved joy.

"You're allowed to want more too," I said.

She blinked, opened her mouth... but said nothing.

We sat in the quiet, both of us weighed down by the ache of unspoken hopes and fears.

And that silence? That was the hardest part.

I MADE A LOUSY MEAL—FISH, rice, and steamed vegetables—the best I knew how. Malia had rested most of the day, but by evening, color had returned to her cheeks. She was sitting up on the settee now, freshly washed and composed.

Even sick, she was beautiful. That warm brown in her eyes. The sweep of her lashes. The soft fall of her hair.

It was wildly unfair.

We ate in silence until Malia smiled at me. I could feel her gaze, even if it wasn't quite steady.

"What?" I asked.

A blush colored her cheeks. "This is delicious. Thank you, Alaric."

"It's nothing," I muttered, embarrassed. "Especially compared to your cooking."

Mine was hardtack. Hers was soft biscuits. No comparison.

She laughed, and something inside me sparked. I'd never made her laugh before.

I wanted to do it again.

"This is the kind of meal whalers eat," I said. "Sometimes worse."

"I'm not a fan of seafood," she admitted.

Shame prickled. I hadn't even asked. I'd just assumed.

"But if you make it," she added, "I think I'd be happy to try it."

"You don't want my food." I grinned, still embarrassed. "If we were ever together, I'd have to learn from you."

The words slipped out too easily. What was I thinking?

But she only smiled. “Then I’d love to teach you.”

She took the dishes from my hands, carried them to the kitchen. I followed, my heart pounding.

She turned, standing close. For a breath, I thought she might kiss me.

“Here,” she said instead. “This’ll get the fishy taste out of your mouth.”

She held out a fork with a slice of mango. I took a bite, oddly thrilled when she used the same fork to eat her own.

Just a fork. A shared fork. But still.

“Mmm. This one’s really sweet,” she said, offering me another. She was already starting to act like herself again. I was glad.

And also not.

Once she’s better, I’m gone.

That was the plan. Always had been.

But then—

What if...

I blinked, watching her hum as she cleaned, sneaking mango slices into her mouth and mine.

The question surfaced before I could stop it.

“You could come with me,” I said, voice low, uncertain.

She froze and turned to me. “You know I can’t...”

My jaw clenched. “Why not? I will protect you. Keep you safe. You would be well-provided for, and would never have to worry about finances or being alone.”

I stepped forward. It was killing me to fight this...

“Why can’t you come, Malia? What are you hiding?”

Her face drained of color, her voice barely a whisper. “If I told you, you’d hate me.”

“Why?”

“I did something terrible...”

"When? To who?" I took another step. Found her hand. Our fingers interlaced, our hearts beating.

"Alaric. You just don't understand. I can't go to Moanalei. I can't go anywhere... if I do, she'll find me, or the witch hunters will find me."

"Who is she?"

Instead of answering, Malia said, "I'm only safe here."

"This place is falling apart. You're miserable hiding," I said, plain and simple, and the hurt reached her eyes. "What are you hiding from? Why won't you tell me?" Frustration welled up inside of me.

She squeezed my hand, but didn't move close to me. Instead, she inhaled and said, "You deserve your life of freedom, Alaric. You don't want to be chained to me, in this dark place with my dark past."

"You don't even want me to stay, do you?" I asked, and her breath caught.

"I..."

Silence.

"Say it, Malia. Please."

"I can't. I can't ask that of you." She shook her head then, then added, "What do you really want me to say, huntsman?"

"You've fallen for a whaler," I whispered and she snapped back, yanking her hand free of mine.

"No, I've fallen for the huntsman, the one who leaves a trail of blood and horror, the one who cares so little for the life of something so large and beautiful, why would he care for the life of something so small and insignificant like me?"

I froze, realizing the weight of her words. "I do care about you. I would do anything for you."

"Except walk away from whaling." She frowned. "You are a whaler. Always have been, and always will be."

Then she shook her head.

A silent moment passed.

She took a breath, as if searching for a change of topic. "Come, Alaric. I have to show you something."

With the tension still thick in the air, she led me to her bedroom.

I froze.

What was she doing? But Malia searched under her bed.

Too dark. She couldn't see anything.

"What does it look like?" I asked, kneeling next to her. My voice was gentler than it had ever been.

Even after she rejected me, I couldn't find it in me to be angry at her.

Because I understood.

Understood that we came from two different worlds. With pasts that haunted us.

But couldn't we work things out?

"It's just a small wooden chest," she said. I found it easily.

After opening the small chest, Malia pulled out a small, worn pouch and carefully untied it. From inside, she drew out a delicate necklace—a chip of whalebone, rough but polished, dipped in deep blue paint. At its center was a faded dark star-shaped marking.

My eyes narrowed the moment I saw it.

Every whaler knew that crew. "That's the mark of the Black Star fleet."

She looked up at me, surprised. "You know it?"

I nodded slowly, voice low. "Not many do anymore. That crew was notorious—drunken nights in every port, riotous living, brutal on their men and even worse to the whales. A cursed lot."

Malia traced a finger along the chipped bone. "My

mother never explained it to me. She just gave it to me one day and told me to keep it close."

My jaw tightened. What had Malia's mother kept from her? If Malia's mother was a noblewoman, what was she doing with a necklace from the lowest of all the whaling crews? "That fleet was lost at sea long ago. My parents argued about my father wanting to join them. It was all I ever heard. Then the ship sank. They say a whale drove its head into the side of the ship, ending its life and the madness. It was good when that ship sank, because the arguments between my parents ended too."

I held out my hand and Malia placed it inside. "Why would your mother give you this?" I asked. "Do you think she was in love with one of those whalers?"

Malia's eyes flashed, a mix of hurt and indignation. "No, no. She was too noble—and vain—for that. And she loved my father–then my stepfather–as far as I know."

She swallowed hard, her voice softening. "I think she remarried so quickly because she couldn't bear the grief of losing my father. He was a good man. A kingly man."

I remained silent. Something was not sitting right.

"But what if..." I pursed my lips before continuing. "What if you were the daughter of a whaler?"

Malia sighed and shook her head. "I'd be ashamed. To come from someone with blood on their hands. But... maybe I've always been the villain in my own story. Maybe my family's full of dark hearts."

I looked at her, steady and sure. "We're not our parents. It doesn't matter where you come from or what they've done. What matters is what you build with your own hands... and your own heart."

I ran a rough hand through my hair, voice softening. "I built my empire from nothing. Nobody believed in me. They said I was reckless, cruel. But I did it anyway. You've got that same fire. Don't ever doubt it."

Her lips curled into a small, grateful smile. She shifted closer and gently rested her head on my shoulder as I looked at the necklace.

"Thanks for coming back," she whispered. "Even if it's just for a little while. I'm going to miss you."

I placed my arm around her, feeling a sudden ache. "I'll miss you too. More than you know."

CHAPTER FOURTEEN

MALIA

I awoke to the sound of wood splitting and metal crashing against something else. Birds chirped and the storm that had passed the previous night left a muggy feeling in the air. As I sat up, my shoulder ached and a shocking sensation passed through my body.

Poison. I squeezed my eyes shut. It had been a rough night, thinking about my strange origins.

Was my mother *really* my mother? Or my father? He had always been kind, though a little aloof. I figured it was because his kingly duties kept him busy.

But mother? She seemed to loathe me the older I got.

As I sat up, my body ached, and I knew exactly what I needed to fully wear off the poison: noni. It was sour and pungent, but it would most definitely help the poison run its course quicker.

That and a walk.

Besides, Alaric was probably ready to go. It was sweet of him to make sure I was alright.

And those sweet words he said to me last night?

I hugged my arms, a sad smile on my lips.

I'd remember it for the rest of my life.

But he needs to go.

We were only making this harder on ourselves the longer we stayed together. So I made a plan: we could walk to town together and then he'd go on his way.

After preparing myself for the day and wearing the last thing I had in my closet–a black lace dress with an elegant corset, ribbons, and long sleeves, I brushed my hair then walked onto the front porch to find Alaric chopping wood.

His shirt was off, the wound on his side a white line. I watched for a moment, quiet. His back faced me. The rhythm of the axe was steady, focused. He didn't know I was standing on the porch and, for a moment, he didn't seem so guarded. He was just... a man. Not a whaler. Not a weapon. Just him.

For some reason, that made my heart ache.

I could almost see a life together: living in a cottage built and kept up by Alaric. Children running around and helping with chores... A husband and wife deeply in love...

And then fear crept in. Would those children grow up to be whalers too?

He paused to wipe sweat from his forehead and that's when he noticed me. A blush crept up my cheeks and I tried not to stare, but I failed horribly. I forgot why I'd come outside.

"Good morning beautiful!" he said, making my heart pound.

"Good morning..." I tried to remember why I came to talk to him. Instead, I stuttered. "Do you always... chop wood... like you're going for a swim?"

He smirked and let the ax have another log. "Do you always spy on men working?"

"I wasn't spying. I was just checking... the weather."

Alaric stopped and rested his elbow on the end of the ax. “And what’s the weather like, Malia?”

My blush only deepened. “It’s hot.” I waved my hand at him. “I’m heading to town today. You better get yourself cleaned up because you’re coming too.”

He only grinned and I hurried in, embarrassed at everything I said. “Hot?” I muttered to myself, shaking my head, trying to reason that it was, indeed, a hot day. And it had nothing to do with him.

ONCE ALARIC WAS ready and we’d eaten a good, albeit a silent, breakfast together, we packed for the brief journey.

“You should go today,” I repeated as I cleaned the dishes, but Alaric gently put a hand on my waist, as if memorizing my shape. My cheeks heated.

“Alaric...”

He was making this harder on both of us.

But it almost seemed like he wanted to... *enjoy* this moment. Our last moments.

“If that’s what you want. But I will walk back with you... to make sure you’re home safe,” he said, then added. “I am a gentleman, you know.”

I laughed, and he rubbed his hand across my back before helping me pack for the journey. He was used to this.

And I secretly loved that he’d paid attention. It was strange... and so new, but I loved it. And I would truly miss Alaric being around my home.

WHEN WE MADE it to town, I used Alaric as a shield against the prying eyes of the villagers. What would I do once he was gone? Everyone would spread rumors about how I’d put a spell on a handsome whaler, and then he mysteriously disappeared. The thought caused my stomach to tighten.

Maybe they won't notice me with him, I thought, though it was in vain. Already a few villagers glanced at me, suspicious.

They didn't say the words aloud, but their gazes said everything:

"Children-eater."

"The cursed girl."

"That poor whaler she put under her spell..."

Alaric walked a step ahead, towering, calm, casual, like he belonged here. He paused at a fruit stand, lifted a ripe noni with a grunt of approval, then began an easy conversation with the merchant. I shrank behind his broad shoulders, hoping the merchant wouldn't notice me.

"That was a good storm last night. Your grove must weather it well to produce such beautiful fruit. That's a miracle in itself."

I shifted back and forth on my feet, eager to get out of there. That was all I needed: a simple noni fruit. So why was he striking up a conversation with the merchant?

The merchant laughed, shaking his head. "There's only one miracle I see here. You're still breathing after heading into the woods with her."

Alaric didn't even blink. He tilted his head towards me, my head down. "She saved my life," he said.

Silence rippled across the market, as if everyone was listening. The merchant looked from me back to Alaric.

"You'd all be mourning if not for her," Alaric added, and a lump formed in my throat. "I'm Alaric Galebourne." Gasps and cheers sounded, something I did not expect. Alaric *was* powerful... The people did not have such a strong reaction to the prince as they did to this whaler. And whaling was illegal here in Corallure. The fact they *liked* him said a lot.

"Whatever you think of her," he said. "You're wrong. And as any of you know, I'm a good judge of character."

"He is!" exclaimed some nearby sailors, lifting their pints to him.

But the crowd began to press in on us. "What did she do?" they asked.

"How did she save you? I thought she ate people for dinner!"

Alaric was bombarded with questions as the crowd grew louder and louder, closing in and somehow wedging themselves between the whaler and I.

A brief wave of panic came over me when Alaric pushed his way through and grabbed my hand. "I've got you." His voice was gentle and did not go unnoticed by the crowd.

"Are you sure she didn't put a spell on you?" asked a woman as Alaric pulled me away.

At this, he turned to her, holding out his palms like he had nothing to hide. "The only spell she put on me was caused by her natural charm."

Natural charm? I blushed while the crowd laughed and found this all very amusing.

And the thing was... Alaric didn't say it like he was defending me, but he said it like it was a fact. Like anyone who disagreed was blind.

My breath stuttered and my cheeks burned. But this time it wasn't from shame.

Not one person argued and the silence shifted. It wasn't quite acceptance, but it was no longer poison. Then he paid the merchant, nodded to the crowd, and led me out of the market, his hand still holding mine.

Alaric took me to the inn where he wanted to check in with his first mate.

"I want to know if they've found the twins," he said. But when we got to the inn, his men looked discouraged and tired. Worn out. From what Alaric told me earlier, they'd been repairing the ship night and day so they could leave Corallure as soon as possible.

I moved to the side of the pub and watched as Alaric spoke to his men.

"Men," he began, voice steady and clear, "this ship is more than wood and sail. It's our lifeline. Our future. Every plank we lay, every nail we drive, we're not just rebuilding a vessel. We're rebuilding our future."

His eyes landed on me, and, though I couldn't confirm it with my bad eyesight and the dim lights of the inn, I was sure he winked. I blushed as the men snickered. "We keep steady, keep working. Because the sea doesn't wait, and neither do we."

I played with the sleeves of my dress and looked around at the men. They were rough in appearance–the years at sea stretching and tanning their skin, their builds large and brawny from the intense labor they did.

But there was something else about them as they listened to Alaric.

They admired him.

They respected him.

For all the ways Alaric was known as a cruel and ruthless whaling leader, it didn't seem that way with his men. Maybe they feared him sometimes, but, in this moment, they looked at him as their leader. Someone they trusted.

And it was then I realized something: *I trust him too.* This was even more shocking to me.

I, Malia, trusted a whaler?

And I love him too. My heart ached as the realization settled in.

"We've weathered storms worse than this. We've fought battles that should've broken us. But here we are still standing, still fighting. So let's show the sea and anyone who doubts us that this crew isn't done yet."

The men erupted in cheers, renewed strength in their hearts.

Afterwards, while Alaric spoke with his navigator, Thatcher, another dark-haired man approached me. It was the same young man I'd delivered a message to and who came to my home with Thatcher.

"I'm Destin," he said, holding out his hand. "Alaric's cousin. I know we've met before, but not formally."

I shook his hand.

"Thanks for saving his life," Destin said. "We wouldn't have gotten far without him, you know?"

I nodded, surprised at the swell of pride I felt inside. I didn't expect it...

I saved his life. And, for once in *my* life, it seemed that my good deed was being recognized. Acknowledged. Appreciated.

"There's something between you, isn't there?"

I jumped at Destin's voice, soft enough that only I could hear. Of course he'd ask that just as I faced the reality of my heart.

A blush spread up my cheeks as I thought of the moment Alaric kissed me. I wanted to say that was as far as *we* went, but that wasn't true.

We held hands.

He kissed my head.

I fell asleep in his arms.

We talked and connected and opened up in a way I couldn't explain.

I felt safe with him, and, I think, he felt safe with me.

He offered me to go with him.

I wanted a life with him... something I never allowed myself to dream of.

"It's... complicated," I said, but Destin didn't seem to mind.

He folded his arms and leaned towards me a little, saying, loud enough that only I could hear, "Alaric hasn't ever spent time with a woman he has with you. That means something, you know."

"He's only trying to protect me." My heart pounded, especially when Alaric looked our way. He raised an eyebrow at his cousin, but continued giving his men instructions and the plans. They all went right over my head.

Alaric promised his men that he would still pay them, still take care of them... something along those lines.

I was trying to pay attention if Destin weren't prying into my feelings.

"If you choose a life with him, he will protect you," he said. "If there's anything I know about my cousin, he doesn't like it when people touch things that belong to him."

"I don't belong to him," I started to argue when a hand rested on my hip. The men were beginning to dissemble and leave on whatever assignments Alaric gave them and he now came to my side.

My heart pattered as self-consciousness flooded me once again.

"You don't?" Alaric's voice was low, like he was daring me.

Alaric's hand was not missed by Destin and he grinned while clapping Alaric on the shoulder. "We'll see you both back here soon?" he asked, a welcome interruption, sparing me from answering the question. "Hopefully the ship will be ready to sail home in a few more days."

With burning cheeks, I looked up at the whaler captain. His hand found mine. "Come on. We better get you back before dark."

So we walked in silence for a long moment, my mind reeling.

He defended me.

He said I am brave.

And now he was holding my hand. Maybe Destin was right... maybe there was something more to this.

Then why don't I marry him and sail off with him?

For just a second, I entertained the thought: we could have a home at the port, where I could stay if he did business off the coast. Or I could sail with him.

And watch him kill whales? That made my stomach sick and abruptly reminded me that I could not marry him. He would just keep murdering the creatures I loved.

Furthermore, I could never live in Moanalei, though I did miss the waterfalls and peaceful forests. But beneath the tropical paradise was a complicated legacy of power and ruin. As soon as I set foot in that kingdom, Sereth would find out and send a witch hunter or guard... I'd be killed without anyone knowing.

As the cottage appeared into view, a lump formed in my throat.

I should thank Alaric.

"Thank you... for earlier." My voice was quiet, but sincere. "You didn't have to do that."

Now that I looked at it, my cottage needed serious

fixing. Shingles had come off the roof, the outside needed fresh paint and stain, and one of the shutters was completely torn off from a recent storm. And when I looked at Alaric, he seemed to notice the same things. His eyebrows furrowed and he didn't look at me as he said, "Don't start thinking I'm turning into a fish out of water." His voice was gruff.

"I don't think you are out of place. I think you're kind."

His jaw tightened, but he didn't let go of my hand. "You don't really know me, Malia."

"I think I'm learning to."

He exhaled and shook his head, though something flickered in his eyes, like I was stripping away a layer he wasn't ready to lose. He began releasing his fingers from mine. "Don't let go yet," I said and the corner of his lip twitched, like he fought a smile.

I motioned to the swing on the porch, the one facing the distant sea, and he nodded. So we sat in a content silence for a while, holding hands, deep in our thoughts.

And in that moment, as the breeze carried the scent of salt and blooming flowers, I felt a quiet strength growing inside me, a warmth sparked by his simple kindness.

He fought for me.

He believes in me.

Maybe I could believe in us.

Another thought came that I never imagined could be mine. But it was: Maybe I could even believe in myself.

CHAPTER FIFTEEN
ALARIC

The noni juice worked wonders. Instead of leaving her, I kept watch on the porch.

Why haven't my men found the twins? I wondered. And where were they? If they were going to hunt Malia, shouldn't they be here by now?

I fell asleep on the porch, dagger in hand.

The following morning, Malia was up before me, humming as she tended the house and made breakfast. I got up and went for a run on the beach. I needed to get my body moving, both to heal my body and, hopefully, my spirit.

I was torn.

Malia.

Or whaling.

It seemed like the answer should be simple.

But a battle raged within.

Instead of heading straight back to the house, I veered into the woods to scout for trees worth chopping.

And then—

Flowers.

She deserved them. I don't know what possessed me, especially when everything between us still felt impossible.

But I wanted to do something kind.

Malia was changing.

Each time she was seen, appreciated, it was like her whole world brightened. Her shoulders eased. Her eyes sparkled like starlight.

She looked like a queen.

I wished I could make her feel that way every day.

I picked a bundle of orange tropical flowers. Didn't know their name, but they reminded me of her.

Bright. Beautiful. A little wild.

After gathering the bouquet and marking a few good trees to cut later, I headed back. Her cottage needed serious repairs.

And maybe... if I showed her I cared—really cared—she might consider coming with me.

Or maybe not.

If she didn't, I still wanted her home to stand strong while I was gone.

Because I'd come back for her.

It was foolish to think that way. If she didn't want me now, who's to say she ever would?

Still... I had to try.

I wasn't used to losing. To waiting. To not being in control.

But for her, I could learn.

I was halfway down the trail we'd walked so many times when my foot caught—

Snap!

I was suddenly dangling upside down.

A curse slipped out, something I'd stopped doing around Malia, but it tore loose anyway.

Grunting, I reached for the borrowed dagger in my boot and sawed at the rope.

It cut easily—too easily. The dagger had truly never been used.

I hit the ground with a thud.

"Oh no!" The voice came from the bushes and I immediately recognized two lanky teenagers hiding. Their voices meshed into chaos.

"We caught the wrong person–"

"He's getting out!"

"We gotta get out of here–"

"Stay where you are!" I exclaimed. "Both of you, or I *will* follow you this time and you will be sorry."

The teenagers froze.

"We thought you left her already," said Lilo, her face pale.

"Who are you both *really*?" I asked.

Niko folded his arms, trying to look brave, but his eyes showed his fear of me otherwise. They knew that, against me, they didn't stand a chance. Especially after what happened last time... "Why would we tell you?" he asked.

"Because if you don't, there will be consequences." I took a step forward and they both visibly flinched.

"We work for Queen Sereth," Lilo admitted. "We're witch hunters. We bring any witches–or those committing witchcraft–to her."

"Why did she send you here, to Corallure?" I asked, knowing full well it was my duty to bring them here.

"She wanted us to search the land and make sure Malia didn't come hiding here after all these years."

I frowned. "So Sereth sent you to kill her?"

Lilo hesitated and Niko glared at her, as if annoyed that she'd shared too much. That was an answer in itself.

"Why does Sereth want Malia dead?"

"It's *Queen* Sereth," Niko muttered, then spoke up. "Why don't you ask the witch yourself?"

"She's innocent."

Lilo and Niko smiled at each other, and a knot began to form in my stomach. They knew something I didn't. But did I want to know?

Yes. It would make it easier to part ways with Malia. The more ugly and unwanted things we found out about each other, the more we would see that a future together was not only impossible, but impractical.

"What did Malia do?" I asked.

"She made the poisoned apple," Lilo said.

I frowned. The poisoned apple? *The* poisoned apple that nearly skilled Sereth?

Rumors said that the stepmother was a witch, which was why Sereth went crazy with the witch hunt after she became queen. Some claimed the apple came from the queen's presumed dead daughter, who vanished years ago.

But nobody had said anything about a *different* witch getting involved.

Malia... That sweet, gentle woman that I was in love with... she couldn't have done this. And then it dawned on me. How many times had she been misunderstood? How many times had people spread rumors and lies about her?

"She's innocent," I said again.

Lilo sighed. "We were there when she made the apple. She's guilty, Captain. Guilty of the poisoned apple, guilty of nearly murdering the queen. You just don't want to admit it."

"She protected you," I fought back. This time, Lilo and

Niko tensed, even looked away. "She did nothing but care for you–probably more than your own parents ever did or could."

"She did," whispered Lilo and Niko sighed.

"Here's the problem." I folded my arms, the bouquet of orange flowers spread all around us. I'd have to pick them up again later. "Sereth gave me orders to take you to the king. So why did she give you different orders? Shouldn't she have given you orders to stay with me?"

They looked at one another, confused.

Now they were understanding.

Why *did* Sereth give us conflicting orders?

There's only one way to find out.

I pulled the sealed letter from my pocket.

Knew it was against the law for me to break the seal.

But Malia's life depended on it.

"Sereth gave this to me. Ordered me to give it to King Halstead when I delivered you both safely to him." I held it up, just to prove it had Sereth's seal on it. Lilo's eyes narrowed and Niko frowned.

To His Majesty King Halstead, Sovereign of Corallure Kingdom,

It has come to my attention that my loyal efforts to secure the stability of Moanalei Kingdom have been undermined by those closest to me—specifically, the twins entrusted with sensitive duties.

Their actions have proven not only disloyal but dangerous, threatening the peace and security of all in the Tempest Seas. Intelligence reports confirm their intentions are in direct opposition to the crown's interests, rendering them a liability that can no longer be tolerated.

I hereby request that Your Majesty exercise your authority to detain and permanently remove these individuals. Their continued existence poses an unacceptable risk, and their elimination is necessary for the preservation of order and loyalty. Their father is gone and their mother's origins are from Corallure. Thus they are under your jurisdiction.

I trust Your Majesty's judgment and discretion in this matter, and expect swift and decisive action.

With respect and allegiance,

Her Majesty High Queen Sereth of Moanalei Kingdom

For a moment, I couldn't speak.

The twins just gaped, wide eyed.

"This is a death sentence," I said.

"She wouldn't," Niko whispered, stunned. Then yelled, louder, "You're lying!"

"How could he?" Lilo snapped back at him. "How could he be lying? We saw papa on the ship! He's not dead... so *she* has to be lying."

And then they argued, their faces red with anger, betrayal, and confusion.

"Stop!" I ordered and they both turned to me. A tear streaked Lilo's face.

I felt sorry for her.

Truly sorry.

"Leave Malia alone," I said.

Niko shook his head. "You're trying to twist all of this. Sereth wouldn't kill us. All she's ever done is care for us."

"She's trained us to be killers," Lilo said, grabbing her brother's arm. "*Malia* cared for us, Niko! She loved us–"

"She would've given us that poison–"

"Niko!" Lilo threw her hands up. "Can't you see?"

But her brother was inconsolable. He grabbed her arm. "Come on, we have to get out of here."

Not before I stopped them. I stepped forward and they both froze. "Don't *ever* show your faces around here again," I said. "Leave Malia alone, or next time you try to hurt her, you will not be so lucky."

"If Sereth hears you're crossing her plans, she might not take it well," Lilo warned, but I didn't care.

"Give me your word–"

"We can't," Niko said plainly. "We don't serve you. We serve Sereth."

Even after they heard the letter? They still didn't believe me?

It was then I realized that, no matter what, Malia might not be safe.

That killed me.

For a moment, I considered my options. It would not be hard to dispose of the twins, right here. Right now.

But I'm not a murderer. That hit me like a storm wave.

How could I ever think that of myself? Because I *was* a murderer. I killed whales for a living.

But not people. I wanted to protect Malia, but I couldn't just *kill* these kids.

She changed me. Perhaps my old self, as scary as it now made me, would've seriously considered ending them right here. I was cruel. I was unmerciful.

But, because of Malia, I became a different man.

"*Get out.*" My voice was low, almost a growl, and they nodded, running away and leaving their trap behind.

When I was left alone in the woods, I rubbed my hand over my face.

Sereth ordered their deaths? Why? Was it because they became more powerful than she?

And then another question arose... *Who* exactly

ambushed us? They bore the Corallure flags, but the king said it was not theirs.

If Sereth wanted to get rid of the twins because they'd become more powerful than her, was there a possibility she wanted to get rid of me for the same reason?

I picked up the flowers, eager to return to Malia.

CHAPTER SIXTEEN
MALIA

When Alaric returned from the woods with a beautiful bouquet of orange lilies, I thought I'd melt. It was the *sweetest* thing anyone had ever done for me. I was so happy, I threw my arms around his neck and hugged him.

And then he just held me.

Our hearts beat against one another, and he buried his face in my neck, inhaling like he didn't want to forget this.

"I need to know the truth, Malia," he said, voice low but urgent. "The poisoned apple. Did you make it?"

My throat tightened. This wasn't what I expected him to ask or say at such a moment. The weight of that secret pressed heavier than ever. "Yes," I whispered. "That's why I'm running. Because of what I did... and what I was."

His gaze softened, but there was something desperate in it. "Who are you really? Don't hide it from me."

I swallowed hard. "I have... connections to Sereth. To the queen. But I'm not who I once was."

He touched my cheek, then rested his hand on my hip.

"Then make it right. Come back with me to Moanalei Kingdom. I'll protect you. I swear it."

A breath escaped me. And just a tiny thread of courage wove through me again.

"You would?"

He nodded. "You can't hide from this forever, Malia. Let's face the past together. I paid my time for nearly killing Sereth." He'd never told me this before. "I served the crown for a few years, and when I earned my freedom I held onto it like my life depended on it. And you can too."

I pressed my head against his chest, grabbing his shirt and sighing. "I'm terrified, Alaric. She won't give me time... she'll just kill me. You don't understand."

"Then help me."

He smelled so good, like the sea and fresh sandalwood.

I remained silent for a long moment. Then... "I need time," I said quietly. "To think. To figure out who I am without all of it weighing me down."

Alaric stroked my cheek. "What about tonight?" he asked. "My men need me, and the Crimson Wake will be ready to sail home soon."

Then he paused. "My men did say Sereth is headed here, but maybe we can meet her halfway."

Just the thought of seeing her beautiful snow white face again caused me to shudder.

"Yes please," I whispered, "just a little time. I'll make up my mind by tonight."

The whaler squeezed my arm. "Thank you, Malia."

ALARIC STAYED AROUND THE COTTAGE, fixing things up. We didn't talk for the rest of the day, and I was grateful for it.

Because I truly did need time to think.

With him, I felt hope.

What if… what if things truly could get resolved between Sereth and I? What if I was free of the burdened past I carried with me?

The sound of the hammer pounding nails, metal sawing through wood, and paper sanding planks filled the air. All of the cottage windows were open, and I did laundry outside, trying to scrub out my thoughts.

Go?

Stay?

His words on freedom resonated with me.

I want freedom so bad. Just the freedom to walk without people calling me names. Without my past haunting me.

As I washed clothes in the front of the house by the well, my mind deep in thoughts, I looked up.

A figure approached from the woods.

Alaric was in the back of the cottage, and I stood, ready to run to him for fear of who the person might be. Did Sereth send someone after me? Was it the assassin? The person seemed rather tall.

But as they got closer, the chestnut hair and shining crown on the head of the prince appeared. His guards were not far behind him, and I stood to greet him.

"Good afternoon Malia," he said and did a little bow while I curtsied.

"Good afternoon Prince Elias." Then my expression fell and my heart began to beat faster. Why was he here? Did he decide I needed to leave, after all? He had always been kind to me, but even he knew what I was capable of…

"I apologize for visiting so unexpectedly," he said, then glanced at the cottage, noticing the pounding noise in the back.

A blush crept up my cheeks. Had Elias heard about

Alaric? Was that why he was here? To talk with the whaler that he and his father hated, because he killed so many whales? Alaric was the reason they banned whaling off the Corallure shores. Alaric's power-hungry business killed hundreds, if not thousands, of whales around here. It was unsustainable.

"It's alright," I assured him. "You are most welcome. Can I get you something to drink or eat?"

He shook his head. "No thank you. This visit will be brief. I've just come to warn you Malia."

"Warn me?"

"Sereth showed up at the port."

I froze. Sereth? Here? Already? Every part of my frame trembled and I tensed to keep from shaking in front of the prince.

"It was unexpected, but she said she is looking for Alaric Galebourne. You know, the whaler–"

"Yes I know..." I bit my lower lip, knowing that Alaric might show up at any moment. He was busy working though.

"She said his ship was ambushed." Elias shook his head. "I mean. She's blaming it on us, but that's all political. I'm here to tell you that she's also looking for you. You are a citizen here and I will do what I legally can to protect you, but I fear she is going to use one thing against you, and I cannot protect you against that act of treason. It can only be resolved in Moanalei, with a fair trial and, hopefully, a fair pardoning."

My heart sank.

"I understand, thank you for letting me know Prince Elias."

He tilted his head. "You can just call me Elias."

I froze. That was *much* too informal. Much too intimate.

"You're a prince–" I began before he said, "And you're a princess."

It was then that Alaric showed up. At the absolute worst timing, when Elias sounded like he was *flirting* with me. My cheeks turned red as a blossomed hibiscus and I swallowed hard.

"Elias." Alaric folded his arms and stood next to me. He was slightly taller than the prince and much larger and muscular too.

Wait... how did Alaric know Elias? Then it dawned on me. Of course he knew Elias! Alaric had saved Sereth's life and she, no doubt, invited him to the wedding. Elias also lived in Moanalei for at least a year, so they must've gotten to know each other while Alaric served his time for nearly killing Sereth.

"Alaric." Elias's eyes narrowed at him, then he looked from the whaler to me. "What is he doing here?"

I opened my mouth to speak when the prince shook his head. "Nevermind. It's none of my business."

"It's really not what you think," I quickly defended myself. "He washed up on our shores and I've been caring for him."

"You ambushed my ship," Alaric said, tense. "You killed some of my men. And you have the audacity to claim it wasn't your ship."

Some of Alaric's men were killed? He didn't tell me that. My heart sank. This was worse than I imagined.

Elias frowned. "We don't attack ships off our coast unless they're doing something illegal." He folded his arms too. "Furthermore, we haven't had problems in the last couple of months so we haven't sent out patrol ships since then. I don't question my men, but I question your integrity. You and Sereth are blaming us, but have you ever thought of your own feud?"

Integrity. That was a crossed line with Alaric. He stepped forward, fists clenched, and Elias's guards quickly stepped forward too, the air thick with tension. "I would never lie–*you* are the coward. You fled the kingdom when it most needed you. I picked up the slack and did what you never could."

Elias raised a brow. "Did you care for Sereth... or did she care for you?"

Jealousy bloomed in me like a bitter root, unexpected and sharp. I knew they had a history. Same kingdom. She probably watched him like a hawk, powerful as he was. But hearing it aloud was something else.

"Sereth fears me," Alaric said. "Just like you do. I've done more for Moanalei than she ever could. Our people looked to you for hope... and you left."

Elias's jaw tightened. His fists curled like strips of koa bark. "You don't know everything, Alaric. You never did. You blame my family, my crown, but your misfortunes belong to you. We're not your enemy. You've made enough of those on your own."

He took a slow breath, then looked at me. "You have to believe me," he said quietly. "And from what I've heard, she's not happy."

"I believe you," I said, dipping into a curtsy, watching as he turned and motioned his men away.

Alaric's gaze didn't follow them. It burned into me. "Who's she? And why did he call you princess?" His voice was all steel and sea wind. "You said there was nothing between you—"

"There's not." I shoved my hair from my face, heat rising to my cheeks.

"Then why would he—"

"It's none of your business!" I snapped, exasperated.

But Sereth was here. She'd come looking for her whaler, only to find out, from Lilo and Niko, no doubt, that I was alive. Now, she would come for me.

If she hadn't already.

I looked toward the cottage, calculating. I couldn't hide for long. Not from her.

"If there's something between you—"

"There's nothing, Alaric. I promise."

"Then why did he call you princess?"

Silence. I closed my eyes, not sure if I could share the truth. "I once was..." I licked my lips before continuing. "I once was of the status that Elias was... but... I think I've since realized I did not belong in that world. Never did. Perhaps my parents weren't even my parents."

"What do you mean?" Alaric frowned.

"I don't think I belong anywhere," I said quietly. "Not to my parents. Not to this place. Not to... anyone."

Alaric's gaze softened, and the roughness in his expression eased into something achingly gentle. "You belong with me."

The words stole my breath. They were said so simply, as if the truth had always been waiting there between us.

I shook my head, not to disagree but to keep myself from falling into that truth. "I'm tired of hiding," I murmured. "I'm ready to face Sereth. To go with you. To... stop running from what happened."

Something in his shoulders shifted. Relief, maybe, or the weight of years easing just a little. But I didn't say I was going with him *for* him. And he knew it.

I stepped back before he could close the space between us. "I should pack my things."

For a moment, he only looked at me, like he was memorizing every line, every shadow of my face. Then he moved closer, his hand brushing my cheek. His thumb traced the curve of my jaw with a tenderness that made my throat ache.

"I'll be with you every step of the way," he said.

"I know." My voice was soft as seafoam. "Thank you." I squeezed his hand.

And then, before I could move away, he kissed me.

It wasn't wild or desperate. It was slow. Anchored. A promise without words. His lips moved over mine with reverence, as though I were something rare, something worth keeping. I kissed him back, my hands sliding into his hair, and for a moment I let myself believe in a world where I could stay.

When we broke apart, our foreheads rested together. My breath trembled against his skin.

"Don't leave," I whispered.

His voice was hoarse when he answered. "Not even the sea could drag me."

And yet we both knew... when I turned to pack my bags, I wasn't really asking him to stay. I was just asking him to help me get through this next trial with Sereth.

CHAPTER SEVENTEEN
ALARIC

She was ready to face her past.

But not ready to be with me.

She never said the word I ached to hear.

Never told me to stay with her.

But I wanted this. Her. A life. Marriage. A future. I wanted to believe staying could be enough.

Still... if I wanted her, but she didn't want me–due to my profession–what could I do?

The thought hollowed me out.

Not to forget the fact she was a princess.

How?

I sat on the front step, my thoughts churning like seawater as she packed her bags.

Was she somehow related to Sereth?

Was she related to Elias?

Can't be. They looked nothing alike, and she had that mysterious Black Star whaling necklace...

"I'm ready." Malia sat next to me on the step.

I placed my hand on her knee and color bloomed in her cheeks.

"I'm going to miss this place," she said softly.

"We can always come back," I reassured her. Malia nodded and placed her hand over my own.

"Shall we go?" I asked.

Before she could answer, she went pale, her head turned so she could see the path in the setting sunlight.

I stood, instincts flaring.

I stepped in front of the witch.

Malia didn't move.

She didn't even breathe.

Lilo and Niko came up the path, followed by two armed guards bearing the blue wave coat-of-arms of Moanalei Kingdom.

"I'll keep you safe," I said, and her fingers curled around my arm.

"Malia, you're under arrest by order of Queen Sereth of Moanalei Kingdom," said Lilo, but the hatred didn't quite reach her eyes.

If anything, she looked exhausted.

"What for?" My voice was rough, and I drew the golden dagger. Lilo and Niko visibly tensed, but Lilo lifted her chin and answered. "For treason."

"What treason has she committed? You have no evidence."

"The Queen's justice doesn't wait for lovesick sailors," one of the guards teased, then both guards stepped forward.

I planted myself between them and Malia. "Not happening."

The first came at me fast. I ducked under his swing and slammed my shoulder into his gut. He staggered, but the second guard was already on me. His fist clipped my jaw, snapping my head to the side. I tasted blood, but I caught his arm, twisted it, and drove my elbow into his ribs.

He grunted, but didn't go down. The first guard lunged again, tackling me from behind. We crashed to the ground, the breath jolting from my lungs. I heaved him off with a curse, my muscles burning. I managed to get both of them on the ground winded, but not out for long.

The teenager girl pulled out a cloth from her bag, and I frowned. What was it?

"Five years ago, Malia was found creating a poison... this one." She held up the cloth. "And she put this poison on an apple, the same apple that poisoned Snow White."

A lump formed in my throat.

I knew this.

"We're going now–together–" I said, "To make things right."

"It's not just an act of treason, but of betrayal," Lilo said. "Malia is Sereth's stepsister."

And then it hit me.

It hit me so hard I stood there, stunned, like a gust of wind had knocked the breath out of me.

It all made sense: Malia had a stepsister. Her mother had remarried and her stepfather had died, leaving her with a cruel, beautiful stepsister.

Sereth.

Why hadn't I connected all of this sooner?

Elias calling her princess.

Malia's ornate dagger.

Hiding her past.

Malia *was* a princess. She would've been the queen had Sereth not stepped up. From what I heard, the queen's only daughter had disappeared years ago. When nobody could find her, it was presumed she was dead. I still remember the black flags they put up around the kingdom to mourn her death. And the weirdest part was that they were only up for a few days, and then everyone moved on, forgetting about it.

Forgetting about her.

Now I remembered the princess's name: Elena Kamalia Keahi.

Malia. Perhaps the kingdom forgot about her, but I'm not going to forget about her. My anger towards Sereth only intensified.

"Malia?" I looked at her.

"I'm so sorry Alaric. I couldn't tell you..." A tear streamed down Malia's face. "The penalty of betrayal is death..."

So she *knew* she was walking to her death with me? She knew, all along. Which is why she never asked me to stay. Never asked me to be a part of her life.

Because she was going to die, and she had finally resigned herself to that conclusion.

Maybe she hoped that, with me, the punishment would be less.

But it was obvious.

Lilo and Niko were here to march her to her death.

"I only meant to help Sereth," Malia said. Another tear streaked her face and her hands shook so bad, she pressed them under her arms. "But it's not what it seems–it never was." And in this moment of vulnerability, the teenagers ran to us. Niko grabbed Malia's arms. I lunged towards her, ready to knock out the boy.

But Lilo came from behind me and shoved the cloth in my face. A distinctly sweet scent filled my nose. It smelled like an apple... at first. But then it became putrid, and almost immediately, the world began to blur.

Malia screamed and fought against the twins.

They gagged her mouth. Tied her hands behind her back.

"Alaric!" she cried, but I was on my knees, unable to move. It was as if the deck pitched below me. I told my body to move, but the strongest sleepiness had come over me.

"Malia..." I blinked. My eyelids were heavier than an anchor dropping to the bottom of the sea.

Malia... I fell to the ground, barely watching the twins drag Malia away before the world went dark.

SMOKE.

As the world came into view, I watched as flames licked the stars above.

It's night? I suddenly remembered everything.

The twins.

The poisoned apple.

Malia.

"Malia!" I bolted up, finding my strength to be exhausted. I felt more sluggish than a drunk after a whole night of ale. "Malia!" I was next to the well.

Must've been dragged there.

Shadows danced across the area from...

I turned to see her cottage in flames. The roof already caved in, and the walls blazed with fire.

"Malia..." Her home. Destroyed.

I pushed on my hands to stand up but froze when the grass felt unnaturally sticky.

Blood. And it wasn't my blood.

My stomach tightened, like a net being hauled in too fast, cutting into itself. This was worse than a shipwreck, worse than watching a man go under and knowing you couldn't save him.

Did they kill Malia?

A scrap of fabric from her black dress sat on the ground. Soaked in blood.

I saw them drag her away... Then why was there so much blood?

They killed her...

No.

No.

No!

I stood and rushed to the house, wondering if they threw her into the flames, as they did before. But the place was ransacked, everything destroyed. And there was no sign of Malia.

Not a body.

Just that scrap of her dress and the sticky blood on the grass.

If they didn't kill her on the spot she was, no doubt, dead by now. They had dragged her away and I'd been out for *hours.* Malia was arrested with the intent of being killed as soon as she reached Sereth.

And the worst part? Malia *had* committed a crime. A *terrible* crime.

It was one thing for a member of the royal family to be threatened by a commoner. But by another royal?

That's why Sereth killed her stepmother...

And now she'd kill Malia. If she hadn't already.

The twins were right.

Anger boiled inside of me: anger at myself, anger at Malia for not telling me the truth sooner, but anger especially that now... we would *never* be together.

She was gone.

Gone!

I kicked a metal bucket, falling to my knees as I let out a scream. My head was spinning, a million emotions kicking in all at once. But the strongest emotion–stronger than the anger and sadness–was grief. Grief because I'd lost her.

I lost her. The one person that had ever become important to me, more important than anything else... and I lost her. I didn't protect her. I didn't open myself enough so that she felt safe telling me the truth.

The whole truth. We could've avoided all of this if we had both been honest–completely honest–about our pasts.

I was an idiot. I had to get out of here. I hurried towards the ocean, knowing it would not solve my problems. But I had to get away from her cottage, away from this situation that was so *wildly* out of my control.

I PACED ALONG THE SHORE, knowing I had to do something. Anything. But what? Malia was a criminal, and even I, as powerful as I had become, could not save her. The most powerful, wealthiest, untouchable whaler in all the seas could not save her.

I kicked the sand and ran my fingers through my hair, frustrated. Furious at myself. Furious that I hadn't discovered her past sooner, or at least confronted her about it sooner.

We could've run away. We could've made it work.

But she made the apple that poisoned Sereth.

I just wanted to believe that she was good, but even she nodded to me that it was, indeed, the truth.

Barefoot, I stepped into the water and let the waves brush past my ankles. The saltwater was soothing, comforting. This was where I could think clearly, where all the troubles of my past and present seemed to disappear. If only for a moment.

The moon sparkled on the water and I now noticed something coming towards me. A boat? Yes, it was a rowboat, with a figure in it.

I frowned. My blood boiled. I grabbed my dagger.

The tall form of the assassin was unmistakable, and when he got closer to shore, he abandoned the boat. I prepared for him, knowing that whenever he surfaced, there would be a fight.

Prince Elias probably sent this assassin, I thought. We did not like each other, and though he said it wasn't his ship that attacked us, I knew better.

Rising from the water, the assassin charged. I barely had time to raise my dagger before his sword came down. The force from blocking the attack jarred through my arms, sending a hot ache into my freshly healed ribs. My grip faltered, and he pressed harder, forcing me back a step into the slick sand.

He swung again, faster than I expected. I ducked, the movement tugging painfully at my side, and barely blocked the next blow. The fight was quick and brutal, but every clash of steel sent another jolt through my battered body. My breath came short, and my legs threatened to give beneath me.

A desperate shove sent him stumbling, and I lurched forward, head-butting him. Pain exploded behind my eyes, but he staggered, swearing. My vision swam.

If I missed my next chance, I wouldn't get another.

Through sheer will, I threw my weight into him, driving him to the ground. My dagger pressed against his throat, my arm trembling with the effort to keep it there. Rage burned through my exhaustion, hotter than the pain.

"Don't hurt me, please!"

"This is the last time you've come for me," I said, my voice a growl. "I've spared you all the other times. Why should I spare you this time?"

His eyes panicked in the darkness of night. Deep down, I was quite impressed that he had the courage to come after me yet again. Prince Elias must have paid him an unimaginable fortune to get rid of me.

"Because she has my family."

"Your family?" I frowned. "Who has your family?" Malia had his family? What was he talking about? This man was a trained assassin... it was odd to imagine him having a family.

"My kids..." And then water pooled in his eyes.

I pressed the dagger. "Speak! Who is *she*?"

"The queen. Sereth."

My hatred deepened. "Sereth?

"She took my children years ago, trained them to become witch hunters. It's my fault for abandoning them—my second wife hated them, convinced me to leave them in the woods to starve. I..." Now he really was crying. "I couldn't live with myself. When my wife died, I found out they had survived. The witch... she took them in. And then they fled to Sereth. She wouldn't let me see them. She wouldn't even let them know I was looking for them." He trembled. "Instead, she threatened to kill them if I didn't do as she said. And she said the only way I could ever reunite with them is if I did what she asked. She sent me to kill you. I've failed time and again, and if I fail again, she *will* kill them."

Didn't she want the Corallure crown to get rid of them?

Reality came crashing down on me.

Sereth.

Sereth? The queen. The woman I had saved five years ago from her wicked stepmother. She framed this man?

"I suppose I don't deserve to live," he said. "We killed your men. We burned your ship."

I released my hold on him and sat back. The man scrambled away, feeling his neck, no doubt where I'd pricked his skin. He let out a breath and sat back, his fingers shaking.

"Your children were on board that ship," I said, trying to put everything together. "Sereth's orders to me were to deliver them safely to Corallure." Then I shook my head. "But you were ordered *by Sereth* to destroy my ship and to kill me?"

He nodded, and, at the same time, understanding poured into both of us. If Sereth sent the ship to kill me and destroy the ship, she *knew* the twins were on board that very ship. Which further sealed the truth of the letter she ordered me to deliver with the twins: she was done with them too. She was trying to dispose of them.

"She was trying to kill my kids!" The man stood and let out a scream, stomping away and grabbing his hair.

I stood too, rubbing my forehead and looking out to sea. My head was spinning: Prince Elias and the kingdom of Corallure were not the enemy at all.

It was Sereth. Snow White.

She's fooled all of us. And then it hit me: if she was so good at framing this man, his children, and me, how much more would it take for her to frame Malia?

Malia, the soft-spoken herb witch who wouldn't ask me to stay because she feared it she was an inconvenience. Who cared more for others than herself.

Water misted the distant air and my eyes latched onto a whale breaching in the dark water. The distinct white tail caused my heart to stir: it was the whale that saved me from the ambush.

I should've died. I should've drowned after the cannon hit.

Yet... I looked up at the stars, and, for the first time in my life, felt something stirring deep inside of me.

What have I done?

My addiction and thirst for power, for control... it released its hold on my heart. All my life, I was terrified of becoming weak–just as my father had been weak–that I was blinded to the truth, to the tender mercies of Akua right before my eyes. *He* had always been in control, not me.

The whale was proof of that.

While everything felt wildly out of my control at the moment, there *was* one thing I could control–and that He probably wanted me to control. And that was me and my choices.

And I choose Malia. I didn't have to figure out all the details about where we'd live, my career, business, working out our differences, and all of that. I loved her, and I wanted to choose a life with her.

If she's still alive. But hope had been sparked inside of me, and the aching to make things right... not just for me but for Malia, this man I just met, the twins, and even Prince Elias.

Elias! I had blamed him for everything, and now he was the only person I could turn to. I looked down at the whale-bone necklace hanging from my neck. For so long I'd held onto this one aspect of my life, not daring to let go.

I'm a whaler, I thought. *A huntsman.* I'd always be one, or so I believed.

But Akua has other plans for me. He always had, and I

didn't know what the future held, but I knew I would give up everything for her. Even whaling. I pulled the necklace from my neck and tossed it as far as I could. It splashed into the water and disappeared beneath, never to be found again.

"Whoa!" I called after the man as he paced, struggling to breathe through his sobs. "Your children are still alive, and we might have time to find them and Malia."

"Malia?"

"The witch whose cottage I was at."

The man nodded and wiped his face. I held out my hand. "What's your name?"

"Jonah." He shook my hand and the enmity and bitterness of our past was resolved, feelings of understanding, compassion, and forgiveness replacing the anger and hurt.

"I have an idea," I said and Jonah looked hopeful. I sheathed my dagger and turned to the island. "And if we can move quickly enough, we might reach them before it's too late." Because I hoped, with all of my might, that it was not too late to save any of them.

CHAPTER EIGHTEEN
MALIA

Darkness.

The ship, where I was imprisoned, rocked back and forth, but I could see nothing. The guards had not bothered to cover my eyes, masking where we were going, because I couldn't see anyways. It was dark, and I struggled to tell where anything was.

But I was sure only a few hours had passed since the twins and Sereth's guards came to get me. Lilo had the scent of the poisoned apple on her cloth and when she put it to Alaric's nose, he passed out.

Alaric. I couldn't stop thinking about him, hoping, praying that he was alright.

And that he won't come after me. He had to move on, had to realize that I was not worth fighting for. Never had been.

Now I sat behind bars, listening to the water lap against the side of the ship.

Tears streamed down my cheeks. My sobs were drowned by the sound of approaching footsteps.

"You were always such a crybaby."

The voice was gilded with scorn, yet carried that infuriating, flirty lilt that Sereth wielded like a dagger.

I wiped my eyes and stepped closer to the prison bars. "And you were always terrified someone might see through you."

Her lantern tilted upward, bathing her in gold light. She was painfully beautiful—snow-white skin, blood-red lips, dark curls cascading like they'd been poured from a bottle of ink. Her beauty had sharpened in five years. It was the kind that could cut.

"The truth," she said slowly, "is that you made a poisoned apple, gave it to your mother, and she brought it to me." Her smile was all blade.

"That's the lie you've been polishing for years." My voice shook, but my eyes didn't leave hers. "Mother never brought it near you. You came to me. Said you needed it to escape her. And then—" my throat tightened "—you used it on yourself when it suited you."

Her expression faltered for the briefest heartbeat. A hairline fracture in a ceramic bowl.

"I did what I had to," she said, voice lower now, stripped of its mocking edge. "Do you know what it's like to grow up knowing you're... nothing? No matter how pretty you are, you're still someone else's pawn."

"Is that what this is about?" I cut in. "You were jealous. Always. It didn't matter what I did. You wanted anything just because it was mine."

The vulnerability vanished like a snuffed candle. "I played the game better than you ever could. And if I had to shatter you to get free, so be it." Her gaze glittered. "That's the difference between us, Malia. You hide when you're hurt. I make sure everyone else bleeds."

I almost laughed, though there was no humor in it.

"And yet here you are, sneaking into a cell to tell me how clever you are. Sounds more like you need my fear to keep you warm at night."

Her grin tightened. "Mother was a fool. She sent that huntsman to kill me. That's betrayal worth burning for. And I made sure she did."

My stomach knotted. I couldn't imagine mother's painful death wearing those hot shoes. "She was still your family."

"You're not one to lecture me on loyalty." She arched her brow. "Speaking of which... I hear you've taken a liking to that huntsman."

My heart stumbled.

"Good," she purred. "Because he'll be dead before the night ends."

My hands gripped the bars. "What did you do?"

"I sent my assassin. He won't stop until Alaric is gone. And he'll die trying if he must."

"No—" Tears ran down my cheeks.

"Cry," she said lightly. "You always were good at that. But crying won't save him. He was too powerful. People listened to him more than me. I couldn't have that."

She stepped close, tilting my chin so we were eye to eye. "You were always too pretty, Malia. Too... good."

"But that's the part you never understood," I said, my voice raw but steady. "Being loved isn't the same as being better. And no matter what you take from me, that's the one thing you'll never have."

Her eyes darkened. "I'll have your crown. That's enough."

"Not if I'm still alive to take it back." I had never considered it. Never wanted it. But now... I knew she could not rule. Sereth's heart had turned completely dark. Unmerciful. Ruthless.

A muscle twitched in her jaw before she stepped back, lifting the lantern. "Tomorrow you'll be drowned."

"Not hung?" I winced. Drowning sounded like agony.

"A witch must sink to truly be gone."

"But Sereth." A whisper. "I'm your sister."

"Stepsister," she corrected, the word flicked like ash, before turning away.

I was left in complete darkness again. I slumped to the ground.

Alaric! He was going to die.

I was going to die.

And there was nothing I could do about it. Except... I hugged my arms. *Akua... help us...* I knew I had done the wrong thing in making the apple. I should've known Sereth long ago. She had always been cruel to me and then that *one* time, when she came, the kids were there, and she seemed so nice. She seemed like she was struggling and desperately needed the apple so mother could sleep while Sereth escaped.

But she lied. And because of her lie, and because I couldn't reveal the truth to anyone who might listen–because nobody listened to me anyways–I was going to die.

That wasn't the worst part though. The worst part was knowing that Alaric was going to die. And there was nothing I could do to stop it.

I DIDN'T SLEEP, tormented as I was about everything: Alaric, the twins, the truth. Sereth had orchestrated everything, except it was all wrong, like a tea brewed with all the worst kinds of herbs.

I thought about how I loved Alaric, and, if things were different, maybe we could settle down and live a quiet, happy life together.

But he loves the sea. He loved whaling. He wouldn't be able to stay put for long.

Then the thought occurred to me. Would he stay if I fought for him? For us? All my life, I ran from a fight. I hid. It was easier.

But what had hiding done for me? I'd lived in isolation for five years, and when Alaric showed up on my doorstep, everything changed.

I changed. I sat up and wiped my tears, feeling like sunlight was pouring into the room, even though it was still pitch black. He showed me I was worth something: tending to me, talking to me, listening to me, even defending me–without a thought–to the people in town.

And then... I looked up. I couldn't see the stars or the sea, but I imagined it in my head.

I'm worth something to Akua. He spared me time and again. How many instances had I evaded my wicked step-sister and survived?

And I'm still alive.

I swiped my hair back and thought about Alaric. He had *easily* overcome the assassin last time.

He can do it again. And, for some reason, I just knew he wasn't dead. He couldn't be. Nobody could touch him...

Except me. A smile crept up my lips as I realized he loved me. He really, *really* loved me. And though I didn't know what our future might look like, especially with our different views of whaling, I had to make the most of these last moments. I had to fight. And so that is what I did.

• • •

I WASN'T sure what time it was, but when footsteps approached, I expected to see the guards. Instead, two tall teenagers stood at the prison doors.

I quickly stood. "Lilo. Niko."

They stared at me, and I could tell they were probably feeling as lost as I felt earlier. But now... Now I was ready to take on the world. For Alaric. For myself. For our future.

"I'm not sure why we're here," Lilo said, then looked at Niko. He couldn't meet my eyes, and I knew it was because of the guilt. They had burned me, thrown me into the furnace and left the house to crumble to the ground. They cornered me, poisoned me, and captured me.

"It's to say goodbye I guess," Niko said, adding, "But last time should've been goodbye."

"We tried twice to kill you," Lilo said. "But you survived. Against all odds."

Another confirmation that Akua had saved me for a reason. "She would've killed you too, you know," I said and they frowned.

"We serve Sereth. She cared for us and took us in when nobody else wanted us. We aren't going to listen to you." Lilo's voice was firm.

I held onto the bars. "*I* cared for you, and the apple you saw me making wasn't for Sereth. It was for my mother, because Sereth said she needed it to escape from her. My mother ended up loathing Sereth, and yes, she did send a huntsman to kill her, but Sereth came to me for the apple. And she lied to you behind my back. She planned all of this."

The twins looked at me like I was crazy. "The ship that ambushed Alaric... that was from Sereth. She wanted you killed."

"She's lying," Niko said. "That ship was sent by Prince Elias and the crown of Corallure."

"No it wasn't," Lilo argued and Niko faltered. "Alaric showed us the letter, and this confirms it."

"It was a setup." I pleaded with them. "You must listen to me. She's not who you think she is. All she wants is power, and she'll get rid of anyone who stands in her way. She sees you as a threat because not only are you both strong, powerful assassins and witch hunters, but you'll eventually become stronger than her. You're getting older, and you'll be harder to control, which she hates."

"Let's go." Niko grabbed his sister's arm, but she hesitated.

"Wait."

A spark grew within me. Lilo was listening and pondering my words. I pushed on. "You are both smarter than this... and kinder. I know who you are because, when I cared for you, you cared for me too. You were just little children who needed to be loved, and I loved you." At that, my eyes watered. "I still do, even if you despise me. Even if you think I'm evil. I would've loved to keep raising you as my own. You didn't deserve to be turned into murderers. You should've been able to have a childhood, like any other child." My heart ached. "And I'm sorry your parents abandoned you. No parent should *ever* do that to their children. Your father searched for you—and he found me instead. He cried because he wished he could go back and never abandon you."

Silence.

Lilo looked at Niko. "See? He is looking for us..."

"But we can't just..." Niko sighed, looking confused as ever.

"I know how you feel," I said. "My mother abandoned

me—maybe not physically, but in other ways. It's why I ran away years ago. I know how that feels."

Lilo's eyes began to water, and I knew she felt the pain, the isolation, the feeling that nobody in the world cared for her. Niko steeled himself, turning away and rubbing his face.

"It can't be," he said to himself, over and over. Then...

"Come on, Lilo." This time he grabbed her arm more forcefully. "Let's go." And she followed him. With my blurry vision I did see her turn once, and I hoped with all of my heart that she would give my words some time and thought. Because, truly, my life might depend on it.

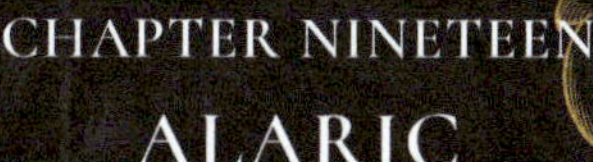

CHAPTER NINETEEN
ALARIC

"After all these years, you've found out the truth, haven't you?" The prince folded his arms. Looked me in the eyes.

"Most of it." I held out my hand. "I owe you an apology, Elias." I was shocked that it was so easy to get an audience with Elias. Even more shocked at how easy it was to apologize. He raised an eyebrow.

"For what?"

"Blaming you for ambushing us."

Elias shook my hand. "Apology accepted."

"But we have a problem," I said. "And we need to act. Quickly."

"Are you going after Sereth?" Elias asked.

My crew stood behind me, ready to help. When we arrived at the palace, Elias didn't keep us waiting, as if he was afraid this was the news I'd share. And now, his eyebrows furrowed when I nodded.

"Her ship is anchored in a bay off the east coast," Elias said. "It seems like she's trying to hide and slip by unnoticed." He walked to the window, where the morning light began to pour in. I knew we were running out of time, and I hoped that Elias might be able to employ horses and ships so we could get to Snow White's ship in a matter of hours.

"I haven't seen her since I left," he admitted. "Just the thought of her makes me sick."

I drummed my fingers against my side. We had to go... now. Jonah, beside me, also fidgeted nervously. We'd been disarmed before meeting with the prince, but he didn't seem concerned at all.

"She's good at that," he said after a moment.

"At what?" I asked.

"Spreading lies and rumors, manipulating situations and making them seem like they're real." He faced us. "I didn't leave her. I tried to work things out. She cast me out and it was in that moment that I knew nothing I tried would help her or appease her. Her mind was set, and she had her way of ruling–a cruel, unmerciful way. I wanted to help the people of Moanalei. I wanted to do more... but she had everyone wrapped around her finger. It was easy for her to frame it in a way that I walked out on her." He sighed. "I don't care about that though. What I care about is that our people are safe. That her people are safe. They've been under her rule for too long. It's time her sister stepped up."

"Malia?"

"Yes. She's the rightful heir."

"She was arrested for the poisoned apple," I said. "Is there a way you can save her?"

Elias pursed his lips. "I think I might be able to... or at least help."

"How?"

"Sereth loathed her stepmother. When things got rocky, she ran to her hidden stepsister–Malia."

He faced the window. "And Malia *did* make the apple. She made it for her mother though, so that she would sleep for an extended period of time. Long enough that others might think them dead, but short enough that the person who bit it would still survive. The whole plan was for Sereth's stepmother to eat it while Sereth ran away, far from the reaches of her stepmother. Malia even promised to help her run away."

That was the Malia I knew!

"But the kids," I said.

Jonah jumped in. "We left them in the woods but she cared for them as her own. I'm forever indebted to her."

"Then why are they so loyal to Sereth?" I asked.

"Because she lied to them." Elias shook his head. "When they saw Malia making the apple, they really believed she was an evil witch who was going to poison and eat them. After Sereth got the apple, she told them to kill the witch. She told them to come to her when they were free."

My insides were sick. How could Sereth do this to them? To Malia?

Elias rubbed his arms. "I'm sure you've seen Malia's scars. They threw her in the furnace but she survived and fled to my kingdom. She remained hidden until I fled here too, not more than a year after my marriage to Sereth."

Marriage to Sereth... that thought made me even more sick. I couldn't imagine what Elias had endured.

His relationship had probably been the worst thing he had ever gone through.

And he looked like he still hadn't healed from it. I felt sorry for him.

As if realizing our dire and timely situation, Elias

motioned to his guard. “Prepare my horses and my ship. We’re going to the hidden bay.”

“Yes, your highness.” The guard excused himself.

Elias motioned to his other guards. “Return their weapons.” I gaped.

“You... trust us?”

“I can see it in your eyes,” the prince said.

“See what?”

“The love you have for these people in Sereth’s grasp.” He nodded, his expression solemn and honest as ever. “Let’s go save them.”

Sereth’s ship was still anchored in the bay, much to my relief. When I wondered aloud why she was still there, Jonah spoke. “She’s probably waiting for me to report.”

Elias looked from Jonah to me. “She’ll be in for a surprise,” he said. I nodded, but no smile formed on my lips. My eyes were riveted on the ship, searching for her, Malia.

We had our plans all ready, and, though I’d only just made amends with Jonah and Elias, I knew I could trust them. I had no choice but to, because if I didn’t, we could lose Malia and the twins.

If they’re not already dead.

No.

I couldn’t think like that. I *knew* she had to be there. I could even sense it...

I’m coming Malia.

I crept down the side of Elias’s ship, hiding near the hull, the sea water spraying me as the ship cruised portside to Sereth’s ship. Now I could see her, barely.

The wicked queen stood waiting for Elias, her eyes dark and menacing, her expression smug.

Sereth had always been beautiful, and it was quite embarrassing that I once had mercy on her for her beauty. It wasn't only that though. I had made an oath to her mother, the queen, that I would kill her, but when I took her to the woods, I knew I couldn't do that. She was too young, too innocent... or so I thought.

And I didn't want her blood on my hands.

Now I do.

Someone was brought next to her and my heart pounded in my chest, only intensifying the feeling.

"Malia..." It was half a whisper, half a prayer. She was pale, wounded, terrified, but proud. Her sleeve was ripped, with dry blood smothered all over it. Perhaps she had given the twins a fight.

That's my girl.

And then I noticed her entire upper body tangled in chains.

Sereth intended to drown Malia, sinking her into the depths of the sea. It was what they did to witches, and it made my blood boil.

Prince Elias stood at the prow, flanked by armed guards. He called out across the water, his voice steady. "Sereth, you are hereby charged with treason, attempted assassination, and unlawful imprisonment of the rightful queen."

Sereth laughed, bitter and dismissive. "You don't have a spine for justice, Elias. You never did." How could she demean him so publicly?

Two figures stood to the side of Sereth and at first their expressions were hard, steely. "You lied to them," Elias said. "You lied to all of us, and this is the end, Sereth."

Lilo and Niko's faces changed from that of anger and numbness to... confusion. Jonah must have appeared next to Elias, but I didn't get a chance to see the rest because I slipped into the water and swam towards Sereth's ship.

When I pulled up onto the bow, I could hear Lilo's voice, cracked with anger and bitterness. "She told us the witch was going to poison us. She didn't say it was for her."

"They're lying to you, darlings," Sereth said, her voice cool. "Don't be ridiculous. Your father *abandoned* you."

"And I'm back to make things right!" Jonah's voice called out. "I've looked everywhere for you, and when I finally found you, she wouldn't let me see you." He was crying.

"I'm so, *so* sorry I left you."

I was getting closer to the deck, knowing that any wrong move could reveal where I was, and that it might put Malia in danger.

Now I could see the twins looking back and forth from their father to Sereth. Niko's fists clenched as he said, "We hunted witches, but we were hunting the wrong one."

And that's when Sereth's face fell, her pale skin seeming to turn even whiter. Lilo nodded to her brother and they turned on Sereth.

Her guards quickly stepped in to defend her, and then it was chaos. The teens were skilled fighters, but they were outnumbered. I jumped into the fray, going straight for Malia when Sereth saw me and screamed. "Get *him*!"

This only confirmed the truth: she wanted me dead. Elias ordered his men to board Sereth's ship, but my crew–experienced seamen–had already swung over. With the amount of people on the deck, and the guards trying to stop me, it was chaos.

Swords clashed.

Men roared.

And Sereth screamed orders.

Then I saw what I hoped would *not* happen.

Desperation.

Sereth dragged Malia to the helm and held her at knifepoint. “Stop!” she exclaimed.

Everyone froze, all eyes turning to the queen’s dagger at her stepsister’s throat.

“Don’t hurt her!” I cried, rushing to the helm but Sereth only pressed the knife into Malia and she let out a cry. A trickle of blood fell down her burn-scarred neck, and I stopped. All time stood still.

“She’s no queen,” Sereth said. “She’s a coward. A blind little thing who hid when her people needed her most.”

I met Malia’s eyes, and even though her eyes never seemed to lock with mine, I knew she was looking at me. A tear fell down her cheek, and, shockingly, I felt my own eyes burning.

I can’t lose her.

We were all at the mercy of Sereth, the woman who brought woes on all of us.

CHAPTER TWENTY

MALIA

"Sereth," I pleaded quietly. "Please... We can end this peacefully."

"Peacefully? Our lives were only ever anything *but* peaceful." Sereth laughed, her flowery scent filling the air. "Once you're dead, my guards will take care of the rest."

"Sereth, *let her go,*" Elias commanded, his hand firm on his sword, but my stepsister laughed like a madwoman.

"My dear *husband*, when have I ever listened to you? You are as much a coward as she is!"

"You've lied about everything," Alaric said and stepped forward. As if warning him to stop, Sereth pressed the dagger deeper into my neck. I cried and he looked like he was going to go crazy because he could not help me.

"Since you're all here, you might as well know the truth before she dies," Sereth said. And she leaned her temple against mine so our faces were side by side. "Don't you ever wonder why mother couldn't stand you?"

"Because I couldn't see," I said feebly.

Sereth grinned. "Oh that wasn't the only reason, sister

dear. She couldn't stand you because you weren't actually her daughter."

My head reeled. What was she talking about?

"You were an orphan dropped at her doorstep, the daughter of a vile whaler and probably some woman on the streets. The queen couldn't have her own children so she took you in as her own. But when you had problems with your sight, she loathed you even more."

A lump formed in my throat.

"How?"

"I read her journal after she died, and the royal family records confirmed that you were, indeed, an orphan."

I gaped, speechless.

"She didn't care for you Malia, and it helped when you decided to disappear. She didn't even mourn the full month for you. The black flags flew for four days, and then everyone forgot about you." Her words cut into me as she said, "You're a nobody, Malia. Always will be."

Elias looked confused, while Alaric's eyes never left me, his knuckles white on the hilt of his borrowed dagger.

A nobody.

I blinked and more tears fell. Sereth was right. Who had ever cared for me? Who had ever seen any worth in me? I looked at the sea, the sunlight sparkling on the water, like glitter dancing on the waves.

"Malia." Alaric's voice was firm, in control, like he always was, but when I looked at him again, I only saw tenderness, as if he were begging me, pleading with me to be able to hear some unspoken words he said.

I love you.

You are the most important person in the world to me.

To Sereth, I was a nobody, which was why she found me easy to bully, to push around. I was a nobody to my mother because I was never hers, and she probably despised me even more for it. And, perhaps, to others I'd met in my flight from home, I was a nobody, a reclusive witch with scars and a dark past.

But I mattered to Alaric.

And I mattered to Akua.

I returned my gaze to the sea, feeling a swell of compassion and light in my soul.

I have worth, I thought. Akua saved me for a reason, and maybe that reason was to meet Alaric and finally discover that worth.

As if in response, something moved towards the ship. It was so silent and sudden, when it breached the surface between the ships, Sereth screamed. Water from the whale's massive body sprayed the area, but it was nothing compared to the giant splash that poured onto the deck, and the rocking of the boat.

It was enough for Sereth to lose her grip on me, and I took the opportunity to distance myself from her. As everyone tried to get their bearings, Alaric was already at the helm. But he didn't stop to help me. He grabbed Sereth and put his knife to her throat.

And just like that, the tides turned.

"Put down your weapons or she dies!" Elias exclaimed and her guards and sailors immediately dropped their weapons.

"I should just kill you," I heard Alaric say. He was seething, but I spoke up.

"Alaric, no!" When he met my eyes, it was almost as if we were going back in time, to the night the assassin came to my cottage. The whaler looked from Sereth to me, a brief second of hesitation, a chance to choose cruelty or compassion.

For a beat, I stopped breathing. I knew he had changed... he had become gentler, kinder.

And then his expression softened when he met my gaze. I let out a breath as he eagerly gave the wicked queen to the prince's guards.

As soon as Elias's guards took Sereth, Alaric was at my side, undoing the chains quickly, his breaths heavy and his fingers trembling.

"Malia." When the chains dropped, I wrapped my arms around him. His hands found me, clasping my sides and then we were kissing. Hard. Desperate. Sure. He was soaking wet, and he tasted like the sea.

I couldn't believe we'd survived. We held each other for, what felt like, not long enough. It would never be long enough.

"Look!" Lilo's voice sounded and everyone moved to the edge of the ship. The whale had circled around before moving back out to sea. As Alaric and I looked overboard, the whale turned its body so its eye gazed up at us.

My whole body stilled as peace enveloped me, like I was being hugged by something even greater than the whale. I smiled and nodded to it.

The moment was so surreal, so peaceful. I'd never seen a whale this close and it looked like it had the wisdom and kindness of a hundred years in its eye.

The whale turned its body and headed back towards sea, the white tail the last we saw of it.

"That one saved me," Alaric said reverently.

"It saved us all." I smiled and felt his hand wrap around my waist, pulling me closer to him.

"You came for me," I whispered. Alaric kissed my temple.

"There's only one person I'm ever hunting for the rest of my life." My cheeks warmed as he rubbed my arm gently.

"Maybe you don't need to hunt her, because she already belongs to you."

Alaric smiled, relaxing for the first time since I'd seen him. He kissed my temple again, then my cheek, then my jaw. I smiled with relief. "You're right," he said. "You *are* mine."

CHAPTER TWENTY-ONE
ALARIC

"Alaric, Malia!" Elias called, and I gave him a look, not thrilled to be interrupted, as we headed down to the deck. Lilo and Niko's eyes were red from crying, and Jonah looked every bit the proud father. Clearly, while Malia and I had reunited, so had they.

A man stood beside Elias, Sereth's first counselor. He looked shaken but gave us both a respectful nod.

When everyone turned to him, Elias motioned for Malia to step forward. She curtsied; he bowed.

"You're not just her sister, Malia," Elias said. "You're the true heir."

Malia shook her head. "You heard what Sereth said. I was a baby, orphaned at birth. I'm no queen. I never wanted that. I also betrayed the royal family with the poisoned apple. Not only must I pay for my crimes, but I'm not worthy to take the crown. I must seek a formal pardon before taking any crown, whether it's my right or not."

"That's fair. And once your crimes have been pardoned or paid, we should let the people decide," Elias said gently but firmly. "I am still married to Sereth so I'm still the king of Moanalei. We can go back, hear their voice, and respect their wishes for their chosen ruler."

He then added, "And we can choose an appropriate punishment for the poisoned apple, though... I think once all things are explained and brought to light, you will be pardoned."

Malia swallowed and nodded. "That sounds fair." Then she added. "But even if the people do vote for me as queen, I don't have the bloodline."

At that, the counselor stepped forward and unrolled a document. "I've served the royal family all my life," he said. "And once someone is recorded as family—blood or not—they are royalty."

He turned to Malia. "You, Malia, are the daughter of a queen. Heir to Moanalei's throne, even before Sereth." The counselor continued. "Your father was a whaler, a member of the Black Star crew. Your mother was a woman at the ports. She died at childbirth, but begged the queen to take care of her child. The queen requested this information be kept a secret, but..." He shrugged. "Since you have all found out, might as well let the world know."

Malia's eyes went wide and she froze, overwhelmed. Maybe even stunned. I watched, my chest tightening as Elias looked at her like she was a miracle.

And then it hit me: Elias was noble. He was a prince–well, the actual king of Moanalei. Malia was a princess. All Elias had to do was divorce Sereth and marry Malia.

He must've loved Malia longer. And now that she might become the next queen of Moanalei...

For a breath, I believed I would lose her. And this wouldn't be the first time. I had just claimed her as mine and now... was I a fool to say such words? A fool to think she'd want me?

My insides twisted.

But then Malia turned to me, searching my face like I was her true anchor. "If I'm fit to rule, I'll only do it," she said, "If you're beside me."

My heart melted right then and there. The flicker of fear dissolved into fierce devotion. Elias smiled at me and nodded. "The people love him. He's already a man of power and wealth." Then he tipped his head to Malia. "A fine choice."

She reached out her hand and I took it, my head spinning. This meant I could become King of Moanalei. That was *not* how I imagined things would go.

The counselor's words had barely settled when murmurs rose from the gathered crew and the handful of Moanalei courtiers who had survived the voyage. Some bowed low to Malia without hesitation. Others kept their chins high, their eyes darting between her and Elias like they were already calculating where power might land.

"It will not be easy," another counselor warned, glancing at me as much as at Malia. "Many in the court feared Sereth but also benefited from her reign. Some will resist your claim. And the people..." he hesitated. "They will want proof you can lead them without falling into the same shadows."

Malia straightened, still holding my hand. "Then I will give them proof. Not with titles or decrees, but with actions."

A young courtier, barely more than a boy, stepped forward. His face was pale, but his voice rang clear. "The docks of Moanalei are already in unrest. Sereth's loyalists will stir trouble when they hear she's fallen." He looked between us. "If you return, be ready for their claws."

Elias nodded grimly. “The throne is more than a crown. It’s a storm. You must both be ready to weather it together.”

I glanced at Malia. She didn’t flinch—not from the warning, not from the weight of what was coming. She met every gaze on the deck with a calm that told me she’d already decided.

“Then we face the storm,” she said.

It wasn’t a coronation. It wasn’t the easy handover of power fairy tales liked to promise. But in that moment, I saw the truth: she was already becoming the queen the people would need. And I’d just promised to stand beside her through both.

And then, like sunlight breaking through cloud cover, a ripple of relief spread through the ship. Several of the courtiers came forward, voices warm, congratulating her on her return and offering blessings for the journey ahead. One older woman clasped Malia’s hands and smiled through tears. “You’ve chosen well,” she said, nodding toward me. “Moanalei will be stronger for it.”

When the twins approached Malia, they all paused.

“We’re sorry,” Lilo said, her voice raw.

Malia shook her head... not in rejection, but in a quiet, knowing way. Her gaze lingered on them, and for a heartbeat, the silence between them was heavy with all the things that could never be undone.

“A part of me will never forget the fire,” she said softly. “Or the fear. Or the nights I wondered if I’d ever wake up again. But I also know the girl and boy I loved are still there. And I’d rather fight to keep that than lose you forever.”

Her voice trembled, but she stepped forward, arms open. The twins didn’t hesitate. They fell into her embrace, clinging like they were afraid she might change her mind. There wasn’t a dry eye on the deck.

Except, well...

Sereth stood to the side, watching everything with hatred in her eyes. The guards were about to take her below deck when Elias stopped them. Just for a moment, they faced each other for the first time in years.

While Malia was overwhelmed with people speaking to her, I watched the interaction between Elias and his wife.

Sereth spoke coldly. “Come to gloat?”

“I came to say goodbye.” His voice was quiet, aching even.

Snow White’s voice cracked, despite herself. “I did love you. Once.”

The prince stared into her eyes, his hand tightening on the hilt of his sword. “And I’ll always wish you had stayed that way.” He nodded to the guards and they took her below. He stood there a moment, looking after where she’d disappeared. Then Elias turned away, and that’s when our eyes locked.

I nodded to him, and he nodded back, but there was something new about him.

He had finally let go.

call.

But the best *and* yet the strangest thing was that Alaric was now my husband. We decided to get married before the journey back to Moanalei, and Elias was more than happy to do a small ceremony on the deck of the Moanalei ship. Surrounded by Alaric's crew, the people of Moanalei that joined Sereth on her journey, the twins, and Jonah, Alaric and I said our vows on the spot.

As I held his hands and looked into his eyes just

moments ago, I couldn't believe we'd gotten this far. That we'd finally made the decision to choose each other.

Even now, sitting with Alaric, his hand on my leg as we watched the sunset, I couldn't believe a girl with such a dark past could have such a bright future.

There was so much ahead of us, including Alaric figuring out his whaling empire.

The Crimson Wake wasn't quite ready for sailing, contrary to previous predictions, but Destin and Thatcher promised to meet up with us back at Moanalei.

"And you better be king," Thatcher teased.

Destin just smiled and gave us hugs. "I'm truly happy for you," he said.

And, before we walked away from them, Alaric turned around. "Thatcher!" he called. "Find that man who's talking about drilling oil from the ground."

"Are you crazy?" the navigator laughed.

"Our whaling days are coming to an end," Alaric said, and I knew he meant it.

So now we sat on the log, husband and wife. My heart reeled in absolute delight and happiness. I couldn't imagine the return journey being separated from Alaric because we weren't married. We'd done enough of that.

A whale breached in the distance and my breath caught as Alaric wrapped his arm around me and drew me closer. It was still amazing to me that this man was in love with me... *Me.* The thought of spending my life with him thrilled me.

"Remember the first night we met?" he asked, breaking the silence.

"Of course."

"You had no idea you'd fall for the huntsman."

"And you had no idea you'd fall for the witch," I teased,

then became somber. "What if the people are afraid of me when they hear the truth?"

He didn't answer with words, but gently turned my chin to face him. The scent of salt clung to his skin, wild and bracing like the sea he conquered as a whaler. He brushed a strand of hair from my face.

Then he leaned in and kissed me–slow and sure. It wasn't rushed, wasn't desperate or chaotic. It was the kind of kiss that steadied my heart, even as it stole my breath. I kissed him back, hoping he could feel my love for him.

When we finally pulled away, he rested his forehead against mine.

My hands slid up against his chest, and I frowned. "What happened to your whalebone necklace?"

"I threw it in the ocean."

"Why?"

"I used to think killing whales made me a man. Gave me control over something big. Something wild and unknowable." He wove his fingers through my hair. I could get lost in his husky voice, soft touches, and sea scent all day.

"When everything else in my life felt like it was slipping through my fingers... the hunt was the only thing I could command. Out there, I decided who lived. Who died. What direction we sailed. I needed that. Control."

"And you still need that?" I asked.

"No. I don't want to control you, Malia. I just want to love you–right where you are."

Before he could kiss me again, I smiled and pulled away.

"Malia." He was eager to shower his love on me, but I had to say, "Well if you *must* know, I told myself I'd never fall for a whaler."

Alaric grinned, his smile lighting up my whole world. Then he said, "It's a good thing I retired." And this time, I let him kiss me. Our lives hadn't been easy, and I knew we had a long journey ahead.

But it would be so worth it.

Because we get to do it all together now.

Gentle puffs of water caught my eye and I pulled away from Alaric to look out to sea.

"Alaric, look." He didn't look immediately. Whales breached in the distance, a peaceful, magnificent moment. I watched in awe, and then... the white tail of one surfaced for a moment.

"That one's been helping us, hasn't it?" Alaric saw the humpback just in time. "He was probably waiting to make sure I did the right thing."

I squeezed his hand. "You did."

The sea shimmered in colors of orange and blue before the sun finally dove below the horizon. And, for the first time in a long time, my heart–my dark, broken heart–felt fully seen. Fully safe... like it was finally going to start healing.

Maybe that was the secret all along. To win a dark heart... you don't conquer it. You love it back to life. And that's exactly what we did.

THE END.

MAHALO!

Aloha! 🌺

If you enjoyed this book, I'd be so grateful if you recommended it to a friend—word of mouth really helps authors like me.

Leaving a quick review on Amazon or Goodreads would also mean a lot. Reviews help other readers know what to expect and help me keep creating stories you love.

As a thank you, here is a bonus chapter–a little peek into Alaric and Malia's life in Moanalei Kingdom. I hope you enjoy it as much as I enjoyed writing it.

Mahalo for your support and kindness!

💙Lei

BONUS CHAPTER

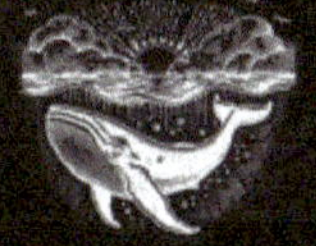

Sea charts and ledgers covered the table.

Destin stood on one side and Thatcher on the other.

I rubbed my chin, trying to soak in all we'd accomplished in just a few short months.

My whaling empire turned merchant trade.

New routes.

New partnerships.

Retraining the crewmen.

And now… a new enterprise: digging oil from the ground.

There were reserves drowning in oil; we just had to find them. The genius from the kingdom of Corallure had more than enough evidence to prove that crude oil could be found in coastlines throughout the Tempest Seas.

And I wanted to be the first distributor of it.

But politics kept me busy.

I'd only been king a few months, and quickly found that it left me little to no time to run my whaling-turned oil drilling business.

Thus I was here, with Destin and Thatcher, putting

them in charge. They were the only two I had complete confidence in while being king and ruling kept me busy.

Yet they seemed off... less engaged. Joking more than usual. Dodging eye contact.

"Are you both planning a mutiny?" I asked, raising an eyebrow, "Or are you bored of all this paperwork?"

"Destin would rather be off looking for that sea witch he always talks about," Thatcher teased, and Destin shoved him.

Then he stared at the maps before us. "We've had offers from the leader of that new kingdom, Alaric."

I folded my arms.

We'd been discussing this merchant and oil business for over an hour, and it took them this long to admit it?

In the northern islands, a new kingdom had formed, one ruled under the shadow of volcano and ash.

Pelehua. The name was as intimidating as the new queen sounded. Rumor was she kept a young princess trapped in a tower, but nobody could yet confirm why.

Prince Elias and his older brother, the Crown Prince of Corallure, were going to investigate. I was sending Thatcher to go along with them. Not only did I want to ensure the Corallure princes made it safely–thanks to Thatcher's excellent navigation–but I wanted Thatcher to create more detailed maps for my businesses.

Now the crown's businesses.

"And are you going to take the offers?" I asked. "We don't know much about Pelehua."

"Except it's ruled by a maniac queen," Thatcher teased, but Destin seemed thoughtful. Serious.

I could tell he was drifting.

"They were good offers."

"Better than what we can offer?" I asked. We were all

practical men, who went for the best deals when they were presented.

But it killed me inside to know that someone else's offer for work–to my two best men–was better than mine.

Their silence spoke volumes.

I nodded, wishing they'd stay, but knowing the call of adventure. That call had urged me to become a huntsman myself. Called me to go to sea.

It was irresistible, and I could see it in their eyes.

"If you go, go with my blessing," I said. "But Moanalei could use captains and navigators like you. Not just on the sea–but here. Helping make the Tempest Seas a better and safer place for everyone."

There was a long pause, then Thatcher said, "We'll think about it, captain."

Before Destin could reply too, a soft knock on the door sounded, followed by Malia walking in with a tray of mangoes, banana bread, salty taro chips, and fresh pressed guava juice.

Destin immediately smiled and turned to me. "Didn't know being king came with snack privileges."

"Is this what happens when you marry a witch?" Thatcher teased. "Food magically shows up?"

"Trust me," I said, wrapping my hand around my wife's waist and pressing a kiss to her temple. "Being married to Malia comes with more privileges than you both could ever dream of."

She blushed while my men laughed, whistled, and hollered.

"Alaric." She gave me a look in her own strange way, her brown eyes and beautiful face the only thing I could ever stare at all day. After we arrived in Moanalei months ago, and the truth was brought to light, the people quickly voted her to be their queen. She was pardoned from her crimes and became the most benevolent queen that the kingdom had ever seen.

"Good to see you, love," I said and rubbed her arm. She smiled, but it didn't reach her eyes.

She didn't laugh at any jokes.

Didn't even try to see me in the way she looked at me.

Malia placed the tray down and wandered to the window, unusually quiet. Normally she loved hearing about Thatcher and Destin's love interests. She even tried to set them up with a few servants.

Not today. She played with her long dark hair and smoothed out her gown, but said nothing.

I took a drink of the guava juice and went over to her while my men began plotting their next plans: where'd they search next for crude oil, and how they'd probably find the woman Destin was sure he loved.

Wrapping my arms around my wife, I kissed her neck, asking quietly, "What's wrong, Malia?"

Her shoulders stiffened and she attempted a laugh.

"Oh it's nothing."

"Nothing." I said the word like it was salty water in my mouth.

The bell rang and Malia sighed. "Time for your meetings, Alaric. You're doing so well at this king stuff, and..." Her voice trailed off.

I took her hands. The meeting could wait. "And you're the best queen this kingdom could ever ask for," I said.

Malia shook her head. Didn't believe me. The bell rang again.

She gave me a quick kiss and then hurried out.

Something is wrong, I thought. And I would find out.

I was king of Moanalei. And the wealthiest, most powerful businessman.

But, most importantly, I was Malia's husband.

I found Malia on the balcony that night, sitting cross-legged in the moonlight, her nightgown loose and long. Her dark hair fell on either side of her, and she absently pinched leaves from a potted herb.

Sitting beside her, I wrapped my arm around her waist and let the silence do the work.

After a long moment, Malia finally spoke. "Maybe some people are right. I'm not a queen."

My jaw clenched and my first instinct was anger.

Who said that? But I kept it in. It could've been anyone who said it–a royal, a commoner, a servant. Anyone. What mattered was Malia.

"You don't need a crown to rule, Malia. You need a good heart, and you have that. Always have."

Silence.

Then Malia sat on my lap and rested her head on my chest. "I just worry that people will always see me as a witch."

"Let them."

More silence.

"It doesn't change your heart. Keep being you, and let people talk. They'll soon see–from the person you are, and your actions–that you're good. Witch or not."

After another long moment, Malia turned my chin and kissed my lips. I'd never tired of these moments.

Heart pounding and calming.

Like anchoring in a bay, finally home.

"Remember, if you can make a rough whaler a better person, you can help anyone," I said.

Malia hesitated, pondering. “Even with my limited eyesight and being an orphan?”

“I think that’s what makes people admire you even more,” I said, rubbing her arm. “I don’t know how you do all that you do with your eyesight. You even stitched me up.”

And then she smiled.

A real smile.

“Thank you Alaric, I love you.”

“I love you too.”

She played with my hair and we sat in silence for a long moment.

Then, “Is everything alright with Destin and Thatcher?”

I pursed my lips then sighed. “They’re thinking of taking jobs under that mysterious Pelehua queen.”

“The one who locked the princess in a tower?” Malia asked, baffled. We’d only heard bad things about the queen, and I was eager to hear the prince's report on her after their voyage.

“I understand,” I said. “It’s the call to adventure. The call for more.” Then I shook my head. “We’re whalers, I suppose. Always looking for the next hunt.”

“Do you want to go back out to sea?” Malia asked.

I hesitated.

Wouldn’t lie to her... because sometimes I did feel that urge, that tug, like a net dragging through the water.

“Sometimes.” Then I drew her closer to me. “But I want to be here with you, more than anything else.”

And then she smiled again. A real, beautiful, angelic smile.

The next day, the princes of Corallure arrived and we held a banquet for them before their expedition to Pelehua.

It was good to see Prince Elias again. He looked healthy and happier than ever, like a weight had been lifted off his shoulders. He and Sereth were swiftly divorced after the crown transitioned from him to Malia. We remained good friends.

And now... we all ate together. The conversation was light. Playful.

"Father says if the queen of Pelehua is young and if–a big if–" said Crown Prince Damien, "Elias is interested, he should propose to her. Strengthen the ties between the existing kingdoms and the new one."

Malia made a face. "You better get to know her first," she said and Elias gave her a serious look.

"Oh I intend to. No more arranged marriages for me." And, though it had hurt him to be married to Sereth, it seemed he could now laugh a little at it.

"We also have to keep an eye out for Destin's sea witch," Thatcher said.

"A sea witch?" Elias raised an eyebrow. Before Thatcher could indulge the princes with Destin's love life, Destin nudged him.

"Let me tell it–it's my story." He nodded to the princes. "Maybe you might have some clues to the location of my mystery witch."

Malia leaned in, all too excited to hear the story again.

"When I was a teen, I met the most beautiful girl in a village here at Moanalei."

"Not as beautiful as you," I whispered in Malia's ear and she smiled.

"We became close friends," Destin said. "But one day a rumor spread. They said my friend cursed a fellow village girl to silence. And so one day the sea witch and her family disappeared."

"What happened to the girl who was cursed with silence?" asked Malia.

"She still lives there. I've asked her again and again where my sea witch is, but she's terrified and won't say a word."

"A mystery indeed," said the Crown Prince, sitting back. Elias was just as intrigued, but thoughtful.

"Your sea witch sounds like a villain, if you ask me," Thatcher joked and Destin rolled his eyes.

"Aren't we all villains in someone's story?" he asked.

Laughter rippled around the table. Even Elias cracked a rare smile.

The laughter faded into a comfortable quiet, broken only by the clink of cups and the rustle of palm leaves in the breeze. That's when Thatcher cleared his throat.

"By the way, Captain—King—whatever we're calling you these days," he said, raising a brow. "Destin and I talked. We've decided we're not staying at Pelehua."

"Too hot," Destin added with a shrug, then smirked. "And too many royals with sharp agendas."

Thatcher nodded. "Besides, you're the one we'd follow into a squall or a banquet hall. You were a good captain, Alaric. You're an even better king."

I blinked. These two had stood beside me through mutinies, storms, and near-death more times than I could count—but this? This quiet loyalty? It meant more than any title.

"You're stuck with us," Destin said, tapping his cup to mine. "Hope you don't mind."

A slow smile tugged at my mouth. "Wasn't really planning on letting you go anyway."

Malia gave me a sideways glance, the corner of her mouth quirked in a smile. She nudged my knee beneath the table, warm and familiar, and I felt it like sunlight through the storm.

I placed my hand on her leg and she quickly grabbed it to squeeze it.

Thatcher leaned back in his chair with a smirk. "If we're staying in court, we'll need new uniforms. Something less fish-stained, more... king's noble captains and advisors."

"Speak for yourself," Destin muttered. "I like smelling like salt and danger. Keeps people guessing."

"Guessing whether you're a sailor or a scoundrel," Malia quipped and I laughed.

"Same thing some days," Destin said with a shrug. "Depends on who's telling the story."

Malia chuckled softly. "To some you'd be a hero. To others, the villain."

I raised an eyebrow. How many versions of ourselves existed out there, depending on the storyteller? I leaned back, one arm resting behind Malia's chair. "Well, I must've done something right. I got the girl.

"Maybe you're not the villain," Malia said softly. "Maybe you were just lost at sea."

My chest tightened... because she knew. Knew how much of my life had been spent drifting, how much I'd tried to outrun the dark past behind me. And still, she chose to anchor herself beside me.

Across the table, Elias lifted his goblet. "To being the villain in one story and the hero in another."

"And to happy endings," Malia added, raising her cup.

And that got me thinking. Maybe Destin was right.

Maybe we *were* all villains in someone's story.

But in Malia's story?

I looked at her, but she was already looking at me in her way, her eyes shining like the ocean at sunrise.

I got to be her happily ever after.

Across the table sat my friends with storms on the horizon: one chasing ghosts, the other haunted by a sea witch.

And something told me that mine and Malia's story wasn't the only one just beginning, but I sure was glad even villains could get a happily-ever-after. Because she definitely was mine.

THE END.

ACKNOWLEDGMENTS

All the glory and thanks goes to God and his son, Jesus Christ. I cannot do any of this without them. I know that Jesus Christ is the true source of peace and only through Him can our hearts truly change. And through Him, we can return to live with God again!

"Come unto me, all ye that labour and are heavy laden, and I will give you rest." -Matthew 11:28

A HUGE THANK YOU to Nicki Chapelway for inviting me to this wonderful collaboration, *To Win a Dark Heart.* What an amazing idea! I honestly had such a great time and adored seeing everyone's creativity and imagination come to life. Everyone in this group has such a unique flair and amazing strengths, and I'm grateful to have rubbed shoulders with each of you!

Thank you to my amazing husband, Jordan. I've grown so much as an author and person, and you've supported me every step of the way. Thank you for your constant encouragement and giving me the time to write and edit these stories. Thank you for always encouraging me to invest in tools and resources to help me improve myself and my craft. You're just incredible.

Thank you to my sweet daughters. I love you both so much!

A special thanks to my beta readers who were so encouraging and helped make this book even better.

And, finally, a huge thanks to my wonderful readers and supporters. I hope this book encouraged and inspired you. Can't wait to share more stories with you soon!

ALSO BY LEIALOHA HUMPHERYS

The Incandescent Kingdoms Series

Married at Sunrise (A King Thrushbeard Retelling)

Hidden at Starshine (A Cinderella Retelling)

Stolen at Alpenglow (A Beauty and the Beast Retelling)

Cursed at Moonlight (A Rapunzel Retelling)

Enchanted at Fireblaze (A Sleeping Beauty Retelling)

Lost at Aurora (A Princess & the Pea Retelling)

Haunted at Twilight (A Hansel and Gretel Retelling)

Poisoned at Dawn (A Snow White Retelling)

These novellas take place in the Incandescent Kingdoms

Prequel Novella

Kidnapped at Dusk (A Red Riding Hood Retelling)

Download this prequel novella free at www.leialohahumpherys.com

The Shattered Tales

To Curse a Black Swan (A Swan Lake Retelling)

Autumn Fairy Tales

Filia and the Fall Festival (A Little Mermaid Retelling)

Hope Ever After

A Beautiful Hope (An Ugly Duckling Retelling)

STANDALONE NOVELLAS

Falling for the Huntsman (A Villainous Twist on Snow White and Hansel & Gretel)

Transformed Tail (A Mashup of the Frog Prince and Little Mermaid)

Ghosts and Ginger Tea (Inspired by the Night Marchers Legend)

OTHER WORKS

Aloha State of Mind

ABOUT THE AUTHOR

Leialoha writes stories inspired by her upbringing in Hawaii, weaving elements of Hawaiian culture, folklore, and setting into her fiction. She holds a BA in English from the University of Hawaii at Hilo and has a deep love for storytelling rooted in place, heritage, and heart.When she's not writing, she enjoys spending time with her husband and kids in the outdoors of Utah. Follow her on social media and sign up for her newsletter at www.leialohahumpherys.com for updates and new stories!

TO WIN A DARK HEART

Want more no-spice fairy tale mash-ups where the villains finally get their chance at a happily ever after? Check out the rest of the To Win a Dark Heart multi-author collection!

Falling for the Trickster by Lucy Tempest (Rumpelstiltskin + Goose Girl)

Falling for the Doomed Bride by C.K. Beggan (Bluebeard + Sleeping Beauty)

Falling for the Winged Witch by Sarah Beran (Wild Swans + Jack & the Beanstalk)

Falling for the Crystal Fae by Anabelle Raven (The Snow Queen + Aladdin)

Falling for the Pirate by Nicki Chapelway (Peter Pan + The Little Mermaid)

Falling for the Mad King by Sydney Winward (Alice in Wonderland + The 12 Dancing Princesses)

Falling for the Sorcerer by Jes Drew (Rapunzel + Swan Lake)

Falling for the Wolf by Megan Charlie (Little Red Riding Hood + Cinderella)

Falling for the Enchantress by Lyndsey Hall (Robin Hood + King Arthur)

Falling for the Pied Piper by Ashley Evercott (Beauty & the Beast + The Pied Piper)

Falling for the Dark Mage by Lucy Winton (East of the Sun, West of the Moon + The Frog Prince)

Falling for the Huntsman by Leialoha Humpherys (Snow White + Hansel & Gretel)

www.ingramcontent.com/pod-product-compliance
Lightning Source LLC
Chambersburg PA
CBHW070839020826
48982CB00022B/1524/J

* 9 7 8 1 9 5 9 1 5 7 2 6 7 *